MW00990028

A City of Brunswik Mystery

by

Leon Shure

* * * *

PUBLISHED BY:

Leon Shure

Littlemayor,

a City of Brunswik Mystery

This is a work of fiction. Names, characters, places, brands, media, and incidents are either the product of the author's imagination or are used fictitiously. The author acknowledges the trademarked status and trademark owners of various products referenced in this work of fiction, which have been used

.

This book is dedicated to Susan and Micah.

There are a few people I'd like to thank: Michael Berger for correcting my grammar and Corrine Levine for reading my first draft. Cover art by Gabi Ladowski

LITTLEMAYOR,
A CITY OF BRUNSWIK MYSTERY

Chapter One

Unavailable, out of the office, touring company sites, in a closed meeting.

We have been unable to contact Severn Matalokus since the Council meeting last June," Tarko, the Brunswik City Manager, told the assembled city officials.

They sat, a wall of men on both sides of the conference table, facing, on one end, the small woman they called "Littlemayor," but never to her face. On the other end of the row was the city clerk, Helena Bell, a woman in her 70's, who looked like she could bite.

Littlemayor was Mayor Martha "Maggie" Philapaitis Wellington, a charismatic, all-eyes-on-her woman, in her mid-60's. Elegantly dressed in a dark blue business suit with her trademark multi-colored scarf around her aging-faster-than-the-rest-of-her neck. Maggie had recently been elected to her third four-year term as Mayor of Brunswik, a suburb on Chicago's wealthy and diverse North Shore, which is, of course, at the Southern tip of Lake Michigan.

"The last thing Matalokus told me," Helena Bell said, "was that the wrecking ball would begin to swing at the strip mall as soon as permits were granted. I issued those right after the June meeting. So far, nothing. The whole building season passed, and now that spring has arrived, still nothing." She looked like she had been personally slighted by a rude individual who deserved to be given rabies by her sharp teeth and infected saliva.

"Worse," Tarko said. "Matalokus has changed his e-mail address. His secretary cannot be reached and only an answering service is taking his messages. Which are not answered. We tried to text him, but he has changed his business telephone number. We tried his home number and were advised that the old number had been discontinued and the new number is classified."

Tarko, an Asian Indian-American, was young to be a city manager. Usually, that job is rewarded to someone of vast experience. The manager makes all the day-to-day decisions for the mostly otherwise employed city fathers. This was Tarko's first managership, having been an assistant in some downstate communities. He was smart and eager and wanted very much to be a success. He looked a little boyish, and the mayor liked him in a parental kind of way.

Maggie leaned forward, which, unfortunately, made her 4 foot, 10 inch seated figure look even more like a child's. "Why would someone who was so gung-ho about building at the corner of Third and Main, suddenly disappear?"

"No idea." This was from Rauptt, chairman of the City's Plan Commission, which had recommended approval of Matalokus' proposal for a mall. To be anchored by a huge single-floor department store, part of a chain of clothing and small appliance stores in the Chicago area.

5

As presented by the developer, Matalokus, the plan was to tear down the present strip mall, combine it with other adjacent lots and construct a complex with storefronts for at least ten other businesses. All in all, the project, also including a few outlying stores in the large parking lot, would upgrade the whole area. The definition of "upgrade" being that the proposed shopping mall on the far west side of Brunswik would provide more much-needed property tax revenue for the city.

Maggie turned to meet the eyes of the Police Superintendent Feather, whose wimpy name belied his aggressive stance and purposely thugged-up speech patterns. "I could, if you want, Madame Mayor, secure and restrain the [wanting to say "perpetrator"] . . . this individual in his home. We know where he lives. Highplace."

Maggie thought, so Matalokus has a home in an even more rich and prestigious North Shore suburb than Brunswik.

Chief Feather continued, "Or I could tap his phones, get all of his tax records, and stake-out his house."

Maggie shook her head, no. "Matalokus is not a criminal or a fugitive. He just doesn't want to be found. I don't want the city to be sued for violating his privacy. I think we'd have a few problems, in any case, doing anything extra-jurisdictional." Adding in case the aldermen did not understand, "Beyond Brunswik city boundaries. I don't want to infuriate city fathers all up and down the North Shore. I just want to know what happened to him. I know, this wouldn't be the first time someone has gotten cold feet on a project, but it is downright strange that nothing has been announced and there's so much secrecy surrounding this man."

She looked at Rauptt of the Planning Commission. "I assume that all the plans could be transferred to some other developer if the proposed project falls through?"

Rauptt nodded, but didn't look happy or relieved.

Tarko took up the presentation. "That puts us in the position of, number one, canceling all of the permits

6

for Matalokus and his company, Severn Holdings. Also this would require Council action to abrogate some significant tax breaks and the rescinding of some zoning and traffic variations. These angered the neighboring sub-division committees in the first place and reversing them now would make us look like idiots. Or number two finding some other company with an abundance of cash to take over the project."

From Rauptt: "Another problem is that this land is in blind real estate trust. It was assumed by the Planning Commission and from hints from Severn himself that the property is owned by Matalokus family members."

His face always flushed whenever he had to speak in public. He was short for a man, only about 7 inches taller than the mayor. He'd retired young after a successful career in business, and, as a volunteer, spent more time on Planning Commission work than did the city's building commissioner or anyone else.

The term "blind real estate trust" caused a few quizzical looks among the aldermen. Rauptt noticed and continued. "A blind real estate trust means the owners are not listed. Their names are not recorded. It's allowed by Illinois law. So no one knows who owns the land. There is a front-man, but he needn't actually be the one who calls the shots on the property. Basically, a blind trust is created so property parcels can be bought up without exciting any interest. which would jack up the price. Also, discourage premature public scrutiny by local jurisdictions. Or so renters don't know who own their apartment building, and, so, can't bother the real owner with calls when the heat fails or a pipe bursts."

Tarko: "We'd need the Severn Company's cooperation in transferring whatever titles or contingencies are necessary to bring in another developer."

Alderman Casey, the chair of the Council's real estate committee, spoke up: "A one-story department store is really needed in that area." Casey was a smooth real estate lawyer, some said shifty. He enjoyed the give

7

and take of politics and could be Mayor some day, many thought. "Otherwise, our residents must travel, inconveniently, to the multi-story super-mall just over the city's west boundary. The area around the proposed mall has one of the oldest resident populations in the city and would get a lot of small bus service from churches and nursing homes."

Maggie decided not to ask how old was old. Was she old? Probably they all thought of her as being ancient. She thought of herself as being in the youth of old age at 66. Maybe they were all waiting for her to die or retire? Too bad, she had a lot of life left in her. She wasn't nearly done yet.

"I don't want to give up on Severn just yet," Littlemayor said. "Has anyone tried just driving to his place of business? Have they gone bankrupt? Has there been any article about the company in the business press?"

"So far as we know, the company is thriving," the city manager said. "It's stock is all family owned, so we can't get as much information from the SEC, but the business takes up an entire, five-story building along Route 88, between Aurora and Naperville. I have personally driven over there, without an appointment of course, and asked to see Matalokus. I was given a polite heave-ho. They said he was in another country."

"I'll take over," Maggie said. "Perhaps my sources will be useful." As Mayor, it was assumed she had access to people with power. Those wealthy enough to own huge North Shore estates and politicians who had been in office long enough to amass both power and wealth. Although the local elections were officially non-partisan, her political allegiance was no secret. She could appeal for help from the elevated levels of the Democratic Party.

Tarko looked relieved at the Mayor's offer but Rauptt looked apprehensive. Rauptt said, "Well, I hope I might help you if you would like someone to bounce ideas around." A bit of a tangle of words. Rauptt added, in explanation, "With."

8

Why, she wondered, was Rauptt taking this problem so personally? Probably, putting the best interpretation upon it, he felt a deep commitment to the city. Maggie made a mental note to put Rauptt's name up for "Volunteer of the Year" and give him a big plaque.

Maggie nodded and smiled at Rauptt to show her appreciation, but her second thoughts were less magnanimous. Did Rauptt fear a loss of status if the Mayor was successful where others had failed?

Was Rauptt interested in being Mayor? She couldn't believe that. He wasn't the type who could project empathy about the concerns of the common voter. Too aloof and specialized. Unprepossessing, not particularly attractive or appealing to the eye.

Quite the opposite from the charming Mr. Matalokus. Dark, handsome, filled with energy, several years older than herself. He had a full head of beautiful white hair. A nice smile. A cute guy. Made her laugh. He was Maggie's type.

The last time she'd seen him, they'd met for a working lunch at the restaurant on the city's golf course. He'd been charming. Maggie was Greek too and felt like she could hear old world music whenever Matalokus spoke.

She'd been a widow for 20 years and a day didn't pass without her thinking about her late husband. He'd been Greek, as well, despite anglifying his unpronounceable Greek name for business reasons.

When Matalokus drove her back to city hall after their lunch together, she'd hesitated in her seat, wondering if he would make the gentlemanly effort to undo his seatbelt, open his door, and circle the car to open her side. Instead, he leaned into her and kissed her fully on the lips.

Chapter Two

Where does one look for a missing businessman?

With the next council meeting three weeks away, Maggie thought she had enough time to make a thorough study, to do all the necessary research, to consider and weigh all the alternatives.

Maggie felt the calmness of being in her natural habitat. She sat in her wood-paneled law office, with law books neatly on shelves, mementos of past cases, framed notes of thanks from grateful clients, and pictures of important friends in high places.

She surveyed the four corners of her desk. She'd never liked an omni-present computer and had traded her desktop for a laptop, which she put in a desk drawer when not in use. She liked to be neat and begin the day with an empty desktop.

Her most recent paralegal, Harper, an enthusiastic second year law student who seemed unusually grounded for a woman her age, was under strict orders to file anything on Maggie's desk at the end of the work day, which could be at midnight. Two file cabinets in the outer office held the papers for all that was current. The rest was in storage. Or, if digitized, downloaded to some remote server for safekeeping.

One cabinet was for her private practice, which had evolved from a specialty of post-divorce child custody litigation to, more recently, child advocacy. Instead of always dealing with the aggravation of warring parents while she tried to protect the children from further harm, Maggie rather enjoyed bullying school districts.

Which must, by state law, provide individualized programs for children with special needs, despite the constant complaints of school administrators about the cost and demands on staff. Maggie also represented a number of charitable agencies for mentally or physically handicapped "special needs" children.

The other cabinet housed voluminous papers concerning current city issues. She'd worked her way up from being a volunteer on multiple Council committees to become an alderperson, then decided to do more, become the boss, run the show, crack the whip. As Mayor of the 35,000 souls in her city on the lake, she often neglected her private practice, hurting the bottom line.

"Harper, I know you're busy preparing filings, but I need you to do some research on Severn Matalokus."

Maggie had already filled her in on his disappearance. Harper poised to pounce on the project. This challenge was out of the ordinary and might give her valuable experience in her own legal career.

Was it a coincidence that Harper was just about the same age as Maggie's younger daughter? The daughter who acted like Maggie was a pariah. Avoided her, withheld visits to the grandchildren? What in the world, Maggie would ask herself, had she done to that child?

"Give me some parameters," Harper said.

"Both the man and his company," Maggie said.

"Certainly," Harper said. "Just the stuff from the Internet search engines? Or everything in the public record? Do you want a written summary?"

"Copies of pertinent documents. You can just present a verbal summary. I want you to also research newspaper archives, even pay to get articles that were written about him."

"How far back? You don't mean from birth? His birth announcement?"

"Why not? We can't know what is relevant. Maybe his past has caught up with him."

"Is he, like kidnapped?"

"I don't believe so," Maggie said, a bit surprised at the suggestion. She hadn't thought of that. Wouldn't there have been a ransom request?

"So, like anything personal?   His parents' obituaries?   Wedding announcements?   Available criminal records?"

"Yes. I don't think he's a criminal. I think Chief Feather would have checked that, but who knows? Drop whatever else you've got going and spend the morning on this."

Harper gave Maggie a quizzical look, but didn't dare probe further into her motives. If she wanted to know about Matalokus, that's what she would get.

Matalokus was second generation Greek-American, according to Harper's preliminary report.

Maggie was third generation. Her family arrived during the Great Depression, moving from Laconia to the bustling life of Chicago's Near West Side. Which had experienced an extraordinary flowering of Greek culture, mutual benefit societies, professional organizations, Greek Orthodox churches and Greek restaurants. A Greek child was taught his Greek, and all about his rich cultural heritage. Family is everything.

From what Harper learned, the Matalokus clan probably arrived after World War II under the Displaced Persons Act and lived in St. Louis. What then?

According to a 35-year old obituary for Severn's father, Severn had a brother, Anthony. No wife was listed for either brother, but that didn't mean that Severn had not married later. She couldn't tell by the order the names were presented who was the older brother.

Maggie could fill in one of the blanks from her own knowledge. Severn had specifically told Maggie, she remembered, that he was a widower. So he must have been married sometime after his father's death.

More information from a longer obituary for the father, written by the newspaper to flesh out the one filed by the funeral home and the family, stated that the man had been a part-owner of a Greek restaurant.

This made Maggie wonder if she'd ever visited that restaurant. Her family had traveled to St. Louis when she was a girl, vacationing on their way to the

Grand Canyon, and her father liked to visit local Greek communities and sample variations on classic Greek recipes.

Maybe she'd even seen Matalokus the father? Restaurant owners in those days were famous for being physically present at almost all times, day or night, to greet and "schmooze" with the customers. An owner would try to remember each patron's name and ask specific questions about each family member. That was how a restaurant became a success, by constant participation of the owner, not by hiring lazy, indifferent managers who would let employees rob the place.

Like her father, Maggie always loved a good Greek restaurant. After Maggie and her husband moved to the suburbs, they found other, closer, Greek restaurants to remind them, lovingly, of their heritage. Highwood, just beyond Highland Park, was the place to go for traditional fare during the precious years before her husband's death.

More about Severn. He must have moved to Chicago after his father's death. Harper found a large number of corporation start-ups and wind-downs with Severn as the managing partner. A lot of legal notices were printed in the back sections of newspapers. Maggie knew that developers are notorious for shallow capitalization, so that failed projects can be abandoned, with enough hidden assets to allow the developer to start again.

No obituary was found for Severn and Anthony's mother. Which could mean she was still alive, although she'd be very elderly, in her nineties. She might be living in the city, enjoying her late life, but Maggie doubted this. Severn would have been proud to tell her if his mother had reached a milestone age.

Thinking back, Severn had never mentioned children, either. That was strange. Everyone brags about their grown-up children, unless they are abject failures or in jail. Also, Maggie had never met a grandfather who didn't carry pictures of grandchildren and who wasn't eager to show them to everyone, whether they wanted to be shown to or not.

Severn's age also put him squarely in the draft for the Viet Nam war. Had he served? He certainly didn't talk about being in the military but many veterans didn't, finding the memories too painful. Severn had been courtly, but Maggie didn't know if his crisp posture, military bearing, and athletic stance were instilled in him by drill sergeants or were the result of a naturally disciplined temperament.

"Here's where it gets really interesting," Harper said. "Look at this." She pushed a printout towards Maggie.

The headline stated: Local Developer Found Dead at Highway Oasis.

A local real estate developer was found dead from gunshot wounds Tuesday morning in the trunk of an abandoned car at the Londisberry Overpass on the expressway, near downtown St. Louis.

Police were immediately summoned by the towing company when the body of Anthony Matalokus was discovered. The identity of the body was quickly established because the victim's wallet, with money still in it, was found on the body.

It is not known, as yet, according to police sources, exactly how long the body had remained undiscovered, but cars aren't usually declared abandoned at the overpass in less than a week. An autopsy will determine the time of death.

Matalokus is a member of a family deeply involved in several suburban developments. It is not known whether his death was related to the creation of these developments and if his death will cause delay in completion of any development.

A family spokesman, Severn Matalokus, also a developer, refused to speculate on any motive to murder his brother and praised him as a forward thinking and honest businessman, who had created several south

14

suburban malls, including Mountolive Spring in suburban Tenton.

When Maggie completed reading this article, dated from almost 30 years ago, she looked up at Harper, but made no comment.

"What do you think?" Harper asked. "Are we going to find Severn Matalokus in some car trunk?"

Maggie shook her head, no, but did not allow her face to show a reaction. Yes, she was a little dismayed, but one must maintain ones cool, calm objectivity. It was just too absurd a thought, in any case, that Severn was dead. Let's not get carried away.

"Did anyone know of the family history when the discussion of the new mall came up?" Harper asked.

"If they did, no one told me," Maggie said. "I had no idea. Someone should have known and advised me. It's relevant information that should have been found through due diligence by the Planning Commission before the city gave its blessing to the project. Anthony's death sounds like some kind of hit by organized crime. Rauptt should have known." Mentally, she canceled the award she'd been thinking about giving him.

"Perhaps Anthony was an innocent victim?"

"I don't think that's even relevant. The death itself should have been a red flag, requiring a great deal of further clarification. Was the murderer ever found?"

"I don't see any follow-up article at all."

What did that mean? That the murder investigation wasn't considered important enough to be presented to the public, or that the backers of Matalokus projects had successfully suppressed any further coverage?

What did it mean that Severn had a family history that included a murder? Maybe Harper was right. This information did boost the odds that Severn's body was already resting in pieces, and that his car was just been better hidden than the one that had held his brother.

Maybe she should order Chief Feather to open all the abandoned cars in the city immediately?

Chapter Three

Where was the guardian of the public peace this fine morning?

Should she catch him in his lair or bring him to the Office of the Mayor in City Hall? Maggie decided she'd go directly to Chief Feather's office rather than give him advance notice of trouble.

She smiled at his administrative assistant, who didn't have the nerve to stop her, and entered through the open door into Feather's office.

She caught him at his desk with his coffee cup half raised.

What is the mystique of a uniform? Feather sat in his blue shirt and epaulets. Maggie had never seen him in civilian clothes. At formal gatherings, he always wore his full uniform, a coat that hid his paunch, and a round hat. He must really enjoy the whole para-military thing, she thought.

Of course, the purpose of a uniform is to set the wearer apart from the normal, the usual, the ordinary. To become a symbol, in his case, of vigilant justice, to warn the wrong-doer that his crimes against society would certainly be discovered and punished.

If Chief Feather had been Chef Feather, how would that change how people think of him, react? What if Feather's fleshy face and burgeoning stomach was under a chef's puff hat and beneath a white smock, perhaps streaked with some soufflé run amok?

Maggie understood that she also wore a uniform. When publicly acting as Mayor, she always dressed up. Would never let anyone see her without her hair well-coiffed and dyed, her make-up hiding as best it could the encroachment of years. Wearing her signature scarf so that no one would mistake her for an ordinary person.

16

If Maggie wasn't in full Mayoral costume to visit the Chief, he might not know who she was and would treat her with the same respect he paid to all miscreants, which was, in short, to assume they'd done wrong and deserved the ill treatment they would surely receive. Throw them in a hole and forget about them.

All of it, this dress up business, was a kind of game. A way to precondition of people, get a specific reaction that leads to a specific result. Opening that person to listening, to be at least courteous, even compliant.

"Good morning," Maggie said, sitting down in a chair in front of his desk, without giving him time to stand up in her presence. She did notice that he had begun to move his bulk upwards, so that was enough. She had elicited some show of respect, then squelched it adroitly by sitting herself down without an invitation.

"Good morning, Madame Mayor."

He really is thinking: good morning, Littlemayor. What can I do for your little toy self today?

"I hope I'm not intruding on any serious police matter," she said. Ha, the city hadn't had a murder in five years. The usual yearly wrap-up of police activities would include a few opportunistic robberies at bank branches in supermarkets, a couple of bar fights, and an occasional high speed chase of a traffic offender.

"No, of course, you're always welcome here." His voice was baritone, but she was sure he aspired to bass.

Feather had been chief for only two years, so still must have felt like he was being judged. The former police chief had served for 30 years. Chief Wolinsky had exercised his option to retire while he still had his health, was awarded a huge pension, and moved to Florida. Smart.

Like Wolinsky, Feather was a life-long officer of the law. He'd risen from a minuscule force in the western suburbs to increasingly prestigious police administrative positions in several towns. He'd first been promoted to chief cop when the sheriff of a far northern county died from arteriosclerosis rather than from a shot through the heart.

Feather had not risen to his current job through acts of courage, but through the whims and favoritism of bureaucracy. In the discussions before Feather was hired, one Brunswik alderman, who liked to think he was a rebel, pointed out that Feather had never actually faced down a gunman. Another alderman said that he himself had never actually died, but was prepared for the journey. "He's an administrator for gawd's sake. Not a frontier lawman drawing down on Billy the Kid."

Littlemayor spoke: "I'm following up on that discussion we had on the missing Mr. Matalokus yesterday. Has there been any new developments, any Matalokus sightings?" Have you searched all the car trunks in the city?

Instead of answering immediately, he asked "Would you like a cup of coffee?" She always accepted coffee, so he didn't wait for an answer, but said "Joyce" to catch the attention of his administrative assistant in the outer office.

He and Joyce had come as a team from his last former job. Maggie wondered how much of a team. She'd met Feather's wife and she was a firecracker compared to him, had a very good sense of humor. Feather probably preferred a less assertive office wife.

"Thank you," Maggie said to Joyce, who had returned with a cup almost immediately. Not a mug that she picked up off the counter, but the special cup and saucer that was kept underneath in the coffee cabinet for just the Mayor. Porcelain. Maggie took a sip. Sludge.

"Yes, it's quite a mystery, isn't it?" Feather said, finally answering the question.

Had he become more jowly? Not more jolly. "I was wondering," Maggie said. "What do we really know about Matalokus? For instance, does he have a police record?"

He took the time to draw in a breath. He must have anticipated her question, she thought. He's

18

constructed what he considers to be a bullet-proof, self-justifying answer.

"I don't ordinarily review each person who deals with the city. After all, Matalokus isn't even a contractee. No one asked me to do a background check on him. I would, of course, have been willing and able to do so." Not my fault.

So Rauptt hadn't even talked to the police chief before Matalokus made that first presentation to the City Council about the proposed mall. Somehow, she'd thought the vetting process was a little more thorough and organized. It would be henceforth.

Feather continued. "Since he's gone missing, I have checked. Nothing indicated he has a police record. Nothing showed that his company has done anything but live up to its commitments. Oh, he was involved in a lot of collapsible corporations when he was younger, but I don't think that's so strange for his profession. His own company has been in existence for a long time now, and I didn't hear any complaints from other cities. In fact, he did do a job or two in one of the suburbs where I served. I hadn't met him, but I hadn't heard anything negative either." So I'd done my part, even if it was unintentional.

Maggie took another sip of awful coffee and put both the cup and saucer down carefully on Feather's desk. Either he really didn't know about the murder of Severn's brother, which meant he was incompetent or he'd decided to take the chance she'd never find out. Probably the latter. After all, it was a long time ago and he had access to police records. She didn't.

"Lots to do, places to go," she said, by way of preparing to leave. "I hope we can always meet for a frank discussion." Make him feel like he's important, as if his opinion counts.

Feather smiled and nodded. Relieved.

The stinker believes he has bullshitted his way through another interrogation by Littlemayor and lived to tell the tale, she thought.

As Maggie walked back through the internal bridge that connected the police headquarters building to

19

city hall, she drew out her cell phone and called Detective Marcus Smith. The amiable, though tough cop. In the few times they'd spoken together, he'd impressed her as having a sense of humor. A rare thing in a policeman.

"Smith here. How may I help you?"

"Maggie here. You know, the Mayor. Would you come over to see me?"

"Sure."

"Just come to my office. Don't announce to the world that you've been summoned by the Mayor."

"Alright. See you in a minute."

Maggie, in her office, took a sip of some decent coffee, made by her excellent administrative assistant, Rosa.

As her cup hit her own desk, Rosa escorted Smith in. He smiled in a friendly way. He wasn't afraid of her. Seemed relaxed. A man without a guilty conscience. How rare.

"How are you, Detective Smith?" she asked. "How's that lovely wife of yours and those adorable children?"

"Just fine thanks. And yourself?"

"Couldn't be better." No need to tell the whole world about her growing concern over the Matalokus situation.

"Am I here to help you root out corruption in the police department?" he asked. "I assume that's because I'm the only honest cop."

Maggie laughed, but had only really heard the word "corruption." She hadn't considered that the Matalokus disappearance had something to do with corruption. She'd think more about that later, she decided.

Enough schmoozing. "I want you to dig up some information for me. No need to tell anyone else." She saw some reluctance on his amiable face. "Oh, it's not national security. You can tell your partner. I just want to know everything available through the police sites about the Matalokus family." Should she mention the murder of Anthony Matalokus? No. It would be her test to see if Smith did a thorough job.

"That shouldn't be any problem. When do you need this for?"

"PDQ." Which in her mind, meant, pretty darn, not dam, quick.

"On it."

That being taken care of, she nodded to Smith, who stood. He did not say goodbye, but looked like he had already begun thinking about his assignment.

Maggie called out through the open office door to Rosa. "Dearie, can you find out if Mr. Rauptt is in the building and tell him to meet me for lunch at the golf club?"

Let's see what lies Rauptt will tell me, she thought.

Chapter Four

The Golf Club restaurant was basically a restaurant for people who didn't play golf. Such as Maggie.

The Brunswik public golf course abutted city hall on one side. All it took to get to the clubhouse was a short trip by car from parking lot to parking lot. No provision had been made for walkers, and anyone who tried to hoof from city hall to the restaurant had to cope with snow in the winter and mud in the summer.

Maggie saw a parked car with a license plate that spelled "Rauptt." She noted, not for the first time, the similarity between the name and an involuntary expression of regurgence. Of all the reasons to change one's name, Rauptt certainly had more than one.

She was reminded again that her late husband had changed an honorable Greek name with far too many syllables to an Anglo-Saxon name with far too many syllables: Wellington, which always reminded Maggie of Beef Wellington.

She realized this was the second time this morning she'd had thoughts connected with food. She was obviously hungry as noon approached. She never ate much breakfast.

Walking through the vestibule, she noticed, with satisfaction, that the storefront of the co-tenant golf shop looked spiffy and inviting, filled with sportswear and golf paraphernalia. From the restaurant came smells of hamburgers and fries and just a lingering whiff of breakfast bacon.

Looking inside, she saw Rauptt's small figure sitting at a square table without a tablecloth. Only in the evening was the restaurant made charming and picturesque with elegant white table clothes and

22

carefully set dishes and silverware. For breakfast and lunch, the casual eater got the diner he settled for.

Rauptt looked around the room nervously. His hands busy, he played with sugar cubes. Several times, he made a tower of cubes, which stubbornly tumbled. He caught sight of Maggie and jumped to his feet, his face blazing red. Embarrassed she may have seen him when he wasn't trying to impress her.

Maggie suspected, that Rauptt, a life-long bachelor, had a huge crush on her, possibly based on her being the only woman in the room shorter than himself. Someone he could make believe he towered over. She wouldn't need to wear heels if he ever had the guts to ask her out, which he never would. She wouldn't have accepted the invitation anyway, claiming there was a rule against inter-government fraternization, albeit unwritten. The real reason she wouldn't accept was because he just wasn't her type. Not at all.

She wondered if he'd be this nervous and wanting to please if she weren't a person in a position of power. Power being, as they say, an aphrodisiac?

In her real life, she was usually overlooked because of her diminutive height. She was quite amused that men might be attracted to her because of her position in city government. The big fish in the little pond of Brunswik. Would she go back to being overlooked once her term was up? Maybe she should run for State Senator, so she wouldn't spend her later years talking only to her cats.

Only belatedly remembering he should help Maggie sit by pulling out and pushing in her chair, Rauptt made a false start, and Maggie sat without assistance. Recovering, he said, "So nice of you to call for lunch."

"I don't think we've gotten to know each other well enough. Volunteers really get the short end and are never appreciated enough."

He smiled. "That's very nice. But I don't feel like a volunteer. I feel like I'm on staff. I put in more than a 40 hour week. I certainly feel like I'm doing my share to protect the city."

He thought he protected the city? Like the town Marshall? Wasn't that her job? "And you really do," she said. Changing the subject abruptly, so he could not brag any further. "What's good today on the menu? You've had a chance to look."

"Luncheon fare isn't elegant. How about a nice half-sandwich and a cup of soup?"

Maggie nodded her approval. Maggie told Rauptt she'd have a half tuna sandwich and a cup of cream of mushroom. Rauptt caught the eye of the waiter. Rauptt ordered for her, which, she supposed, was a gentlemanly thing to do, but which somehow rankled her. A bit presumptive of an inability to order for herself, like she was a child.

Rauptt had a whole corn beef sandwich and chicken noodle soup. The waiter said he'd be back with the soups right away.

Maggie looked at Rauptt. He was perhaps 10 years younger than herself.

That meant she was in fourth of fifth grade when he was born. Why was age such a big deal that it had an effect throughout life? Age should be irrelevant, not determinative of relationships, outside of family life. Her level of energy was obviously higher than his even though she was older.

Also, Rauptt was a detail person but bad with people. She was only somewhat of a detail person but was a people person through and through.

The waiter brought their soups. Hers was less than boiling hot, but tasty all the same. She didn't see any steam rising from Rauptt's soup, and he didn't look too pleased about it.

He isn't being assertive about sending the soup back, she thought, because he doesn't want to fit the stereotype of being a picky old bachelor.

Putting down his spoon in disgust, he said, "I've been giving the Matalokus project a lot of thought since the meeting yesterday." Maggie was relieved Rauptt had brought up the subject first, not wanting to appear to be scolding him over the failure of the project to materialize.

24

"And what do you think?" she asked. "I've been wondering what steps are taken by the Planning Commission to assure that these things go smoothly."

"I believe we did all the pre-planning necessary. I thought it was a worthy project, good for the city and good for tax revenues."

She wanted details. "What is done, typically, when a developer comes in with a plan? I think I served on every other city commission before becoming an alderman, but not on the planning commission."

"First of all, Matalokus Holdings has a fine reputation. Severn, the person, brought copies of his proposals for successful projects in other cities. Actually had a scrapbook of his press clippings and print-out of articles from the Internet."

That's not really reassuring, she thought. No one brings in their bad clippings.

Rauptt went on. "Even though I'd never worked personally with Severn, several of the commission members had positive things to say about him, citing past experiences. Such as, finding one of his completed mall projects well designed. The world of developers in the Chicago area is like a club in some ways, and reputations are fragile. Nothing I heard, and I did check with other planning commissions in other towns, indicated anything but that Severn Holdings is known for its integrity."

She nodded to close the subject, although she was not satisfied with the answer. Another thought. "I'm not quite sure how to ask this," she said.

"Just tell me your concern, dear lady."

What was this "dear lady" stuff? When had he begun to call her that? She was sure she'd let him get away with saying that, sometime in the past. Her polite unwillingness to shove the expression down his throat must have seemed like tacit agreement to its use. Too late to stop him now.

"Do such large projects, not this specific project of course, but projects of typical developers and builders elsewhere lend themselves to irregularities? I mean, I don't want to seem naive. I imagine that, in some cases, not in Brunswik of course, a significant amount of money changes hands on the big projects, if you know what I mean? We do live in Cook County, after all." She meant the county with the worst reputation for corruption in the State of Illinois, possibly the world.

Rauptt looked blank for a moment, then appalled. "Oh, you mean bribery? Corruption? Kickbacks? Does it ever happen? I'm sure it does in other suburbs, but I'm personally not someone who would tolerate such activities. And if I found out, I would certainly report any such to Chief Feather, who is an ad hoc member of the plan commission."

This was meant to satisfy her, but didn't. What exactly were the safeguards against bribery and corruption? Who watched out for crooks?

Not him. He was the monkey who saw no evil. Did he think everyone felt the same way about corruption as he? That corruption could not happen because no right thinking individual would ever tolerate such activities?

Look who she was asking. Maybe he was, in his own mind, an incorruptible official, but what about anyone or everyone around him on the commission and in city government? Were they all like him, the gold standard for personal honesty?

It's easy to honest, she thought, if you're rich like him. He made his money years before or inherited it, wasn't being crushed by a mortgage and wasn't supporting a brood of lazy children and a wife who needed a new dress for every occasion.

"I'm also troubled," she said, "about the lack of knowledge about who actually owns the property. For instance, who owned the property before the Blind Trust began its work? Who are the owners of the present strip mall?"

He made an I-can-answer-that expression on his smug face. "In some cases, tenants of the strip mall probably own their stores in a kind of condo agreement, with an overall management responsible to them, which owns a small percentage of the whole as payment. Or the

26

tenants were long-time renters from an owner who didn't want to be bothered by daily complaints and who hired a management company."

A long answer is usually a sign of ignorance. Why not just say you don't know?

"As for the undeveloped land needed for the project," Raupt continued, "the properties, I believe, were still owned by the families of the German farmers who first settled in the area or was land bought by investors of the railroad."

All well and good, but who were the actual owners? What were their names and who were the investors in the new project?

Maggie struggled with the complexity of the transactions. Contingencies, contracts, coordination with the city. When did ownership actually transfer? Why couldn't anyone just say: These are the people who presently own the properties. And the project at the end would be owned by these particular investors, who would make an enormous profit. Enough to fill the trust funds for their as yet unborn great-grandchildren.

"Would you mind doing some checking? I suppose the original project didn't ring any warning bells, but now that a problem has developed, I'd like to know, backed by the history of the properties, the history of titles, from the Title Companies or the Country Recorders Office. To the extent, it's possible to know. I'm imagining that these sales were contingent, wouldn't really occur, until the project received city approval or the actual start of the project. Also, there must have been rights of first refusals that may have required registration with the county."

She got a nod from Rauptt which meant he would find out what he could. He didn't seem at all pleased with the assignment.

Why?

How did she know that Rauptt wasn't himself the owner of the property involved?

Chapter Five

"It's a pleasure playing phone tag with you," Gene Casey, the alderman, said.

Maggie was finally at home in her downtown Brunswik high-rise condo. She'd been calling, back and forth, leaving messages at various numbers the Alderman had specified as places he could be reached during the day. Every time Casey returned her calls, she'd been unavailable herself. And so the game continued.

Maggie had returned to her law office at about 3 p.m., handled some of the legal work for the day, talked to some clients, then decided after an hour she'd be more comfortable working in her third, much less pretentious and a lot more comfortable, office at home.

"Yes, thank you for calling back. You certainly are a busy man. I called your office, the title company, and, I hope you don't mind, I even tried your residence. How many cell phone numbers do you have?"

"More than three, less than six. Some are personal, for the family, some are so my constituents can leave me nasty messages, night or day."

Maggie heard a disconcerting number of clicks and a mechanized voice said "Louise Hutchins." Call waiting, or, more accurately, call-interrupting tried to break into her conversation.

Little-white lying by Littlemayor: "Uh-oh, one of my constituents is trying to reach me, so I know exactly what you mean. Please wait while I find out if it's important. If it's something I have to do immediately. Just stay on the line." She didn't wait for his consent. She was the mayor and a lady, and it was her prerogative. She pushed the "flash" button on her phone. "Hello!"

"Maggie, hello. It's Louise. How the hell are you? Your office, Rosa said, you went home early. Are you alright?"

"I'm fine. Just wanted a quiet place to think. Look, I'm on the line with an alderman. I want to talk to you. Can I call you right back?"

Louise was Maggie's best friend. They'd gone to private school together as children. Louise became a prominent psychologist, known for her books and her appearances on late night television, where she simplified complex concepts for a breathlessly waiting public. She'd become a spokesperson for psychology and for scientific research in general. Mostly, though, she was invited back because of her acid wit. Made as many enemies as friends with her sharp tongue.

"Yes, I'm on the east coast for one of the shows, plugging my new book. You've got my cell number?"

"Yes. I'll call you right back. I promise."

"Good because I worry about you."

"Bye for now." Maggie broke that connection.

She pushed the "flash" button to, hopefully, reconnect. "Gene? Are you still there?"

She heard nothing. What did people do for frustration before telephones? They married young.

Maggie broke the connection and heard telephone buzz sound. She pushed more buttons and saw the number Gene had used to reach her. A number that wasn't on her list, even though it was constantly updated, so she could reach city officials in emergencies. She wrote the number on the pad she kept by her phone, for future reference.

She pushed the right buttons and heard the comforting "beep-beep" high and low sounds, which meant she was again placing a call.

He picked right up. "I don't know what happened, but suddenly I was disconnected. Sorry, the same thing happens to me if I use one of these damn buttons."

"Damn" was mild compared to some of the language she heard that would have offended her mother. If people said 'fuck" in front of her, they usually

29

apologized, but they weren't embarrassed enough not to use the word again in their next sentence.

"Gene, while I've got you on the line, I'm still thinking about the Matalokus problem. I know you were involved in liaisoning, if that's that a word, with the Plan Commission for the full Council.

"Yes, but you know, I try to be two people in this kind of case, wear two hats. I try to make sure the commission recommendation is presented as clearly as possible, but also I try to keep some objectivity as an alderman who will help make the final decision. You know, I bring up the recommendation of the commission, under Council rules, and the recommendation is a motion that doesn't need to be seconded. That doesn't mean I won't help in picking apart a proposal or in vigorously questioning a builder."

"Yes, and I appreciate your hard work." How much ego-stroking did these men need? "What I'm curious about is who gives you input about a project like the one we're talking about?"

Was that too subtle a question? Maggie didn't want to ask the more direct question: who have you been shooting your mouth to about this project? Who did you forewarn so they could screw this up?

Gene was a person who everyone knew. He was slowly building the political and social networks that would allow him to run for mayor someday. He might even leapfrog over that job to challenge Maggie if she decided to run for State Senator.

He had a growing reputation among the party elders, even on the state level, Maggie knew. His successful real estate firm handled listings for the rich and political elite and his legal work made the whole process of buying and selling a single easy process. He must have made a fortune, she thought, helping banks foreclose on mortgages during the business downturn and in selling those properties when the economy improved.

Maggie didn't know how much Gene was personally involved in any particular aspect of his practice. She suspected that most of the detail work was done by his administrative assistants. That left him plenty of time to wheel and deal.

She'd done her share of real estate closings as a young lawyer, taking any business that came her way or accommodating relatives. She might have done more, made herself an expert in real estate law and practice like Gene, but found the work with desperate parents and their children, who needed her protection, much more fulfilling.

When Gene remained silent, Maggie decided to try to get her answer from a slightly different angle. "To put it another way, when a project is proposed, who are the people you might consult with? I'm talking theoretically here." She knew Gene might not want to share the names of some of his cronies and business partners. Because it was just none of her damn business.

"You mean, what advisers do I have when I'm trying to make up my mind about a project?"

"Yes."

"I might for instance, call the chairpersons of local homeowner groups. Management companies. Other real estate firms to see how things are selling in a particular area. Call some constituents who want to be advised about things proposed for the community. Talk off the record, deep background, with the newspaper owner, not the editor. Call the county officials, call the state representative for the district. More often, just to chat than to lay some proposal before them. Just do a little groundwork. Make sure everyone who might have an interest can get a hearing so he won't object when it comes time to make a decision."

She realized Gene's network was just as extensive as her own. That gave her some pause. Maybe, Maggie thought, I should be grooming someone, not Gene, to take my place when I stop being mayor. She felt Gene was too self-centered and greedy to be a good mayor, too smooth, too willing to prosper even if it meant hurting others financially. She should find someone else, someone she could mentor, to be the next mayor.

She said. "I'm having some trouble knowing who are the big players in the Matalokus project. Who owns or owned the land? Who are the major investors? Who stood to make money and who might want to prevent the project from happening? Maybe you could help me with the last question first. Who was against the project?"

He considered her question. "There's always some naysayers. People don't like big projects around their corners of the world. Afraid of traffic, afraid that strangers will come into their communities and fling around beer bottles at midnight. Afraid their influence over local zoning will decline. That bars will be placed near schools and churches."

Wanting to provide more details, without actually answering her question. "Then there are the people who simply want no change. Don't want even want light pollution. Like their area dark and quiet. Don't want the police concentrating on shoplifters instead of arresting phony charity solicitors who prey on the elderly. Don't want their children to be attracted to a mall, where they might meet even naughtier children. Where they will see goodies they will beg their parents to buy. I think that doesn't begin to cover it. There are the real lunatics, the xenophobes, the anti-modernists. You must deal with the same people."

"Yes, what I'm trying to figure out is who was the most against the project."

"I don't think I could narrow it down like that. Maybe a ringleader on a subdivision homeowners committee? Someone the media would seek out as a negative voice to balance off a positive report?"

Frustrated that she couldn't get real, useable and helpful information. "Could you give it some more thought, and see if there is someone or some group you could identify that would make the most trouble?"

"If that's what you want. But you aren't supposing that someone in this city went out and knocked Matalokus over the head? Really, I don't think we're facing an armed rebellion."

Chapter Six

Where the fuck [oh, pardon my French, Madame Mayor] was Louise?

Maggie redialed five times in the course of an hour, but wherever Louise had gone, she wasn't answering her cell or had abandoned it in her hotel room. Not typical of Louise. Once she got an idea, such as "find out what Maggie is up too," she usually would doggedly pursue her pursuit to its completion.

Unable to talk to Louise, Maggie did the next best thing and called Suzanne Ashley, Louise's daughter. Suzanne, a psychologist, had recently relocated to Brunswik from the city with her two lovely children and her awful husband, Ash, who taught at the University.

She was much less acerbic than her mother, except on the subject of her mother. Suzanne chaffed under the criticism of her in Louise's books. Her mother used Suzanne as a bad example, only barely covering up the identity of her daughter by using fake names.

Maggie felt that Suzanne, unlike her own younger daughter, was an example of a daughter who got along with her mother, as best she could, despite disliking her.

She still had no idea why her own daughter hated her. Maggie often tried to guess what she'd said and done to her then adolescent daughter that had been so awful, but always drew a blank. So far as Maggie could recall, they'd only had the typical mother-daughter conflicts as a daughter asserts herself into adulthood.

"Suzanne, it's Maggie. Have you got a minute?"

"Maybe. [Voice withdrawn from the phone, "Oh Sera, must you?"]

"Is Seraphina being a handful?"

"She is." Maggie contemplated the never ending chain of mother-daughter conflict stretching back to cavewomen and cavedaughters.

"Sue, I was talking to your mother, when I received another call and then when I got back on the line, she was gone and I can't reach her."

"I know she's on a talk show in New York. Maybe the taping is going on now."

Maggie envied the sweet life of being teased by some handsome, graying late night host on national television. Feeling that intense interest. What a thrill it would be to dress up for the show and make an entrance to the sound of clapping.

"So you don't know of any reason, anything that might be bothering her?"

"I'm sure," Suzanne said, "that she was just checking on you."

"I suppose. Well, as long as we're talking, how are you? How are your gorgeous children and Ash?" Nobody liked Ash. He was a know-it-all, even if a brilliant man.

"Ash is Ash. The children are growing. Especially Seraphina, becoming the person she will be. I feel a little overwhelmed about her. Whether I can provide any guidance, or whether I will repeat all my mother's mistakes."

Suzanne is such a wonderful woman, Maggie thought, maybe I should be mentoring her to become the next mayor? The question was, though, would people accept a psychologist as a politician?

She couldn't think of any example of someone who'd made that leap. Plenty of physicians were in Congress. It's one thing to accept a healer of broken bones, another to accept a healer of broken brains. Just being a patient of a psychiatrist or psychologist could ruin a political career. Even in the 21st century.

Perhaps, though, Brunswik was the exception, could accept a therapist as a scientist and leader. The average education in Brunswik was so much higher than the national average. A very sophisticated electorate.

Even if people would accept a psychologist as a politician, Suzanne had the extra problem of having an obnoxious husband. Would voters overlook unlikeable

Ash because Suzanne was personally well liked by everyone? Her marriage to Ash shouldn't be held against her. Suzanne was outgoing and public minded and was a fine public speaker. She was generous with her time and often spoke on subjects of recent interest, such as drug addiction.

Maggie decided to give this mentoring idea more thought.

Call interrupting announced that Maggie had a second call, from Tarko, the city manager. Here I go again, she thought. "Suzanne, dear, I have another call. I'll keep trying to see if I can reach Louise. Why don't we meet for lunch? I'll have my administrative assistant call yours."

"Great."

Maggie pushed the "flash button" and heard Tarko's voice.

Maggie liked Tarko. It was his old eyes and boyish face.

In the personal interview she'd held with him, she'd been barred by law from asking some questions that would have satisfied her curiosity about his life. She couldn't ask anything about his age, political affiliation, or religion. Or his sexual preference. Maggie agreed that this was the right stance to take, to treat everyone equally. In any case, she knew that Tarko was married to a woman, but, as yet, had no children.

Besides, someone could learn a lot from a resume. For instance, she'd been able to guess Tarko's exact age by when he graduated with a degree in city management, and how many years he'd spent in managing other cities or villages.

Tarko was also someone she could mentor. Maggie didn't think, however, that he wanted to be a mayor. He was on the fast track for city managers. He was young, had risen fast and could look forward to serving in much larger and prominent cities. Just not the largest, like Chicago, where the "strong mayor" concept still held sway. City managers served, usually, because most smaller towns and suburbs, like Brunswik, couldn't afford a full time mayor.

All the administrative work fell to the city manager, who, in theory, made no public policies, but carried out the wisdom (ha!) of the elected officials. In reality, city managers proposed much of the policy adopted and provided a professionalism that didn't necessarily reside among the public officials.

"Hello, I'm here. I was on another call. What can I do for you?" Maggie, through necessity, used that short sentence to stop people from meandering all over instead of simply stating their reason for calling.

"Hello, I'm glad I caught you. Are you out speechmaking?" Tarko knew that Maggie's weekday nights were often filled with Parent-Teacher meetings, homeowner groups, the League of Politically Minded Women, the Chamber of Commerce, Men's Dogooder societies, and even with church groups who wanted to weigh in on current issues.

"No, for once, I'm home." She didn't mind talking to Tarko, but knew this wasn't a social call. "Are we in some unexpected crisis?" Which was another way of saying, "What can I do for you?"

"No, maybe part of a crisis. After the meeting about Matalokus, I called by opposite number in his town, Highplace. I know the city manager there from conferences and conventions. A nice, older guy."

How old was old, Maggie wondered.

Tarko continued. "Probably in his last manager position before retirement. He speaks his mind, not caring about further recommendations. Anyway, I asked him about Matalokus. I probably should have called him long ago, but I don't like to spread local gossip."

"I quite understand. Did this man . . .what's his name?"

"Frank."

"What did he have to say on the topic of interest? Does he know Matalokus?"

"Yes, has had many dealing with him. Likes him. Respects him."

"That tells us something, right there. Does he, by any chance, know where Matalokus is?"

"Unfortunately, no. No one has seen him."

"Wait," Maggie said, "you mean, someone has stood outside his home to see if there is any activity?"

"Apparently. He leaves his garage every workday, but no one can see through the tinted windows of his limo. The limo returns in the evening. Also, no one has filed any kind of missing person report about him. "

"I'm finding this very hard to believe. If he's as wealthy as we imagine, wouldn't he have people cleaning his house, people taking care of his lawn? He obviously has a limo driver. Prominent people don't just disappear like the homeless. People who work for him at home or at the company must gossip all the time. How can someone be present in his home and at work, and no one has seen him or will talk about him?"

"Matalokus apparently demands a lot of loyalty from the people around him. If he wants to lay low, he can do so, and no one is going to say anything."

"Do we know if anyone is living in his home with him?" She took a breath. "For instance, his wife?"

"No, he's a widower. Which doesn't mean some woman or whoever isn't living there with him. Or that his adult children, if he has any, aren't living there occasionally."

"Does this Frank fellow have a theory of what's going on?"

"Not really. He can't guess. For some unknown reason, Matalokus doesn't want to be seen or contacted by anyone."

Obviously. Maybe they could reason this out together. "Let's think. For what possible reason would someone disappear?"

"I've been thinking about it. Avoiding someone, avoiding something. Preventing something from happening or not happening."

Chapter Seven

Maggie did not want to ring Helena Bell's bell. The prickly city clerk obviously didn't want anyone to ring her bell either. Maggie stood at the counter of the City Clerk's office.

"Helena, I wonder if you can supply me a copy, not the original of course, of the Board meeting recording from June of last year, the meeting where Matalokus made his final presentation? I've already got the minutes for the meeting."

Helena nodded, wordlessly, walked over to a cabinet and, turning her back to Maggie, began to search for a DVD of the meeting. Maggie wondered if Helena's expression had soured even further while not observed, if that were possible.

Finding the disk shouldn't be a problem, Maggie thought, and should present nothing to further anger the chronically testy Mrs. Bell.

To Maggie's surprise, Helena needed to examine a large number of DVD's. These should have been in some order, even if the filing system was only understood by her. Nine years times 12 meetings a year. Beginning the first year of Maggie's administration, so about nine years ago, Board meetings were recorded and broadcast over the city's cable access channel.

The intrusion of cameras was bearable considering the positive consequences. The public had a right, she'd reasoned, to see its representatives in action. Another positive was that everyone acted with more decorum if they knew their every expression could be seen.

Also, the male aldermen and city department heads shaved their five-o'clock shadows, and the women alderpersons and administrators wore more make-up and dressed up.

A good thing, Maggie thought, that, as part of the agreement negotiated during her first mayoral year, the city demanded a free cable channel for public events in return for a monopolistic utility franchise agreement with the cable company. Some Brunswik residents actually watched each council meeting like reality television.

The camera seldom lingered on Helena during meetings, fearful, Maggie supposed, that wrinkles were contagious.

Maggie knew Helena was angry at her because she had the temerity to be younger. Jealousy? Bitterness about what the years had done to her?

Sorry about that, Maggie thought. I really should have realized when I was born 10 years after you that this act, not voluntary on my part by the way, would be so offensive.

Maggie again wondered how Helena had ever been elected to office. The only possible explanation was that Helena had once been less cantankerous and was even able to smile during her first election campaign. That, however, was 25 years ago, and Helena, the old lady, was no longer a middle-aged candidate who could point to her civic accomplishments as leader of the League of Politically Minded Women. She was still the city clerk because everyone had grown up with her in that role, and no one else really, really wanted the job of a drudge.

Was it age? Not everyone grew worse with age, did they? Maggie wondered if she was nine years less pleasant than when she first presented herself to voters as a choice for Mayor. Maybe. In the last election, she'd strained occasionally to maintain an interested look as speaker after speaker voiced conventional wisdom. Was her patience waning? Probably.

How about her love of people? Let's say it had declined to the "like very much" level. She promised herself she would make every effort to keep from sinking to the "kinda-like" level.

Thinking about Helena, Maggie wondered if she herself was becoming a different person. Not just getting older, actually metamorphosing into someone else.

An inevitable process. She'd been several people already. First a baby, then a toddler, a young girl, an adolescent, a young woman, a mother, a lawyer, a middle-aged woman. Each time, those around her treated her as if she were an actually different person, another person. This wasn't reincarnation exactly, but it was disturbing.

She was going to be old lady Maggie and there was nothing she could do about it but die, which she had no intention of doing soon. She was from a long-lived family and had good genes. The problem wasn't continuing with her life. It was remaining a person who people took seriously, not a satire, a self-parody of herself, as she grew old.

Behind her eyes, she was still the same young girl who'd readied herself for life, laughed, grew, learned to take care of herself, became the mate of a fine man and mother to her children. The same one who finished her law degree and opened her practice, lived and became an honest politician.

The laughing child was present throughout, but, increasingly, no one else could see her. Oh, sure, the people she'd grown up with, like Louise, still saw the laughing child. Unfortunately, those who knew the real her inside, were becoming less and less numerous and one day, sadly, only she would vividly remember that person.

No one could fight it. Something in the brain, something in human programing, changed the pluses to minuses as one grew older. Not just with her, everyone. The impression, the first thing people thought about someone else, was dictated by something complex in the brain. Young, slim, even features, and the arrow pointed towards positive. Old, fat, nose less than ideal, and the observer's opinion was in the default negative. Maggie was entering the negative zone, for sure.

"Here it is. I made several copies after the meeting. You may keep this one."

Maggie was surprised. This was very civil of Helena. "Thank you, thank you very much. Oh, not to take too much of your time, but do you have the sign-in sheets for that meeting? A copy will do nicely."

This drew a short clipped nod from Helena, as if she worried she'd been, albeit briefly, too nice. She drew out the sheets from the same folder in her hand and went to the copy machine.

Clutching her purse, the sleeve of the DVD, and the papers, Maggie walked back to her city hall office.

She received a pleasant greeting from Rosa, which was made even more welcome by its contrast to her reception by Helena.

Maggie put the DVD in the player, turned on the television monitor she mostly used to see election results, and leaned back in her chair, which reclined about 30 degrees.

Familiar faces popped up on the screen. Maggie was seated in the center of a long desk, a dais, for the six aldermen, herself, and Helena. Maggie only voted in case of an aldermanic tie.

Maggie found watching herself to be disorienting, like she was in two places at once, and didn't at all like the way she looked, the image being so different from the way she looked in the mirror while getting ready for a day's work.

The handsome face of Matalokus appeared in profile. He sat at a table in front of the alderman and city officials. Also at the table were Rauptt and the city engineer, who was present to answer questions about traffic impact. Also, the city attorney, a young man, in his second year in that position, who was very eager and bright.

Was she right about Matalokus' age? That he looked about Maggie's age, perhaps a little older? One can tell most easily when a person is about one's own age, but guessing the age of those much older is an art. To the teenage ticket-sellers at the two Brunswik movie complexes, Maggie must have looked like an escapee from a nursing home, but to another 66 year old, she probably looked young.

The camera swept the audience. Many had turned out, interested in knowing how the city council would vote on the project. Such as those nearby homeowners desperate for the status quo. She recognized a representative from the local Chamber of Commerce, who had spoken out in favor of the project.

Becky Frangelmore, the reporter, was there, taking notes furiously. Looking a little bedraggled, as if she'd been so rushed to get to the meeting, she couldn't adequately comb her hair. She looked a bit like a Fury.

Maggie liked her. Becky was always trying to write the best, most thorough possible, report on any issue, no matter how dull.

To Maggie's surprise, several unexpected people were also in the audience. She'd been too busy at the meeting, looking at her papers and anticipating questions from the alderman, to recognize who else was in the crowd.

Surprisingly, she saw Benjamin Edelton on the DVD images. He was the aide to the speaker of the Illinois House, Steven O'Malley. Why in the world was Edelton there? He was gray-haired, prematurely, but was, Maggie guessed, in his early 40's. He didn't look bored. He hung on every word Matalokus uttered.

Another person whose attention was riveted sat in the first row of the audience. She was a slim woman, elegantly dressed. Put together, every hair in place, as Maggie's mother used to say. This woman wore jewelry very inappropriate for the occasion, as if she wanted to draw attention. Even so, Maggie hadn't noticed her. She was probably in her late 40's, early 50's, still very attractive, just slightly too old to be a trophy wife.

On the screen, after a particularly difficult exchange with the most negative alderman, Merit Berger,

Matalokus turned around to catch the eye of the mystery woman, and they shared a moment of frisson.

Who was she?

Maggie sorted through the sign-in sheets. Many familiar names appeared, each one creating a brief snapshot in her mind. People she'd met over the years. People who had a specific problem with an issue.

Yes, she'd been right about Edelton being there. In the space next to the name for the address, Edelton had written "Springfield, Illinois," the state capital, and next to it, the largest town from the district served by his boss, O'Malley. The address, written tightly because there remained so little room, was probably for the Speaker's district headquarters. Maggie wrote down the address. A phone number was also provided by Edelton. She also wrote that down.

So who was that woman?

Maggie scanned for women's names and no name jumped out as being the woman in the first row. She tried again. This time, she saw, in handwriting she didn't recognize, the names "Mr. and Mrs. Severn Matalokus." In a women's handwriting.

Chapter Eight

Should she call the Speaker or his aide to find out what concern the mighty might have about the Matalokus project? She doubted his aide would be open and honest. Better to try to catch the big fish.

She'd met the Speaker, O'Malley, several times and had spoken to him twice. The first time was trivial and the second allowed her to have a career in Illinois politics.

The first time, she'd eaten a hot dog while talking to him at the annual party picnic downstate. He'd been witty and charming and told some great stories about Illinois politics that only an insider would know.

The second time, he was member of a panel of the Democratic Party's state central committee that interviewed her and other potential candidates. This was before she decided to run for Mayor, and she might not have thrown her hat in the ring, if she'd received a negative rating.

The mayoral position in Brunswik is officially non-partisan, but, she was proud to present herself before the committee as a member of the Democratic Party, which plays such an important role in Cook County in the assimilation of each wave of immigrants.

The interview was like pre-approval for candidates. A winnowing process. To decide whether and which potential office holders were stupid, insane or otherwise unacceptable and who might have a political future.

Tacit party approval of the party was all she wanted. Which meant the local pols would recommend her to the precinct captains, who would push her campaign literature. Allow her signs on lawns of the faithful.

She was thrilled when she received the party's unofficial endorsement to run for Mayor.

Her impression of O'Malley at the time was that he was impressed by her. Of course, she was younger then and full of litigious fire. O'Malley was an older man at the interview, and he'd be in his 70's now.

She summoned up a mental picture of O'Malley. He looked Irish, if there is such a look. The only distinguishing feature she could imagine was particularly Irish was a kind of thin upper lip that almost disappeared in a shy, humorous smile. She thought at the time of the interview that O'Malley found her attractive, in a kind of spider-eats-fly kind of way. Or wolf eats doe. Better analogy, Big Bad Wolf eats Red Riding Hood.

She'd talked to people in his office about party matters since that first interview. O'Malley wielded great power in the party, and, of course, in the state's House of Representative. In many ways, he was more powerful than any sitting governor, because governors come and go, and, horrifying to even imagine, might not be a Democrat. Someone like O'Malley persisted forever. No legislation, even the bills proposed by a Democratic governor, passed the House without his approval.

His family was also active in politics, and it was rumored that his son-in-law might become the next state Attorney General, which would be fine for O'Malley. He'd have a lot of influence with the state's chief investigator of crime and corruption.

Thinking about crime and corruption, how honest was O'Malley? In a state where graft was an art, he must have been a master. "Pay to play" is what some called it. Spend enough and spread it wide-enough and a lawyer, for instance, could find a safe perch as a judge. Spend even more and an egomaniac CEO could run for governor.

Maggie called the number from the sign-in sheet and asked to speak to O'Malley.

His secretary almost laughed at her.

What was her name again and how was it spelled? Rep. O'Malley was on the floor of the House and she could submit Maggie's name if he cared to stop and respond to whatever she wanted. What did she want, anyway?

That drew Maggie to a halt. The question, really, was "what was O'Malley's interest in Matalokus and/or his project?" but she hesitated to say that directly. Even if she reached O'Malley, there was no reason to think he would willingly be honest with her. She wanted to phrase her question, lawyer like, so the answer would reveal more than O'Malley wanted to tell.

She could make some guesses about his interest in Matalokus. Maybe O'Malley saw Matalokus as governor material? Or was it that O'Malley himself was a secret owner or investor in the mall project and would he make a lot of money if it went through? Maybe O'Malley even knew where Matalokus was hiding.

Losing patience, the secretary said, "If you'd like I could try to reach one of his aides."

A good suggestion. "Is Mr. Edelton in today?" Maggie had little confidence Edelton would tell her what she wanted to know, if he knew anything to tell. She might have gotten a spontaneous response from a surprised O'Malley, but aides know not to speak for their bosses without strict approval.

"Yes, he's here, but he may be in conference." "Conference" being the washroom, in most cases, or out to get a drink. "Hold on, I'll try to connect you."

And so the runaround begins, Maggie thought.

Maggie heard telephone noises. "Mr. Edelton's office."

"May I speak to Mr. Edelton?"

"Whom may I say is calling?"

Maggie identified herself, emphasizing the words "mayor" and "Brunswik." The suburb was not the biggest in Chicagoland, but was prestigious and rich and had a famous university. Also known as a headquarters for many charitable organizations and for some large insurance companies. A U.S. Vice President had come from Brunswik long ago. Serving under which President, she did not remember.

"Could you spell your name?" Maggie spelled her surname out, slowly, one letter at a time. She repeated the spelling once more. She spoke out the name "Wellington" after, as if she were in a spelling bee.

"And he can reach you at what numbers if he is unable to answer your question right away?"

Maggie carefully spoke out the numbers for her offices. She began to doubt she'd ever reach Edelton and wished she'd had the foresight to ask Rosa or Harper to make this call. To spare her the humiliation of a snub. Too late to start over, she thought.

"I'll try to connect you," the voice said.

More telephone sounds, and a click. "Hello, Edelton here."

A surprise to actually reach him, but, still, not the friendliest of greetings. He could have said, "Maggie, how nice of you to call!"

"Hello, it's Maggie Wellington." When she heard nothing in reply, she said "Mayor of Brunswik."

"Of course, of course, I know who you are. Nice to hear from you."

Like she really should be calling more often? "Yes, it's nice to hear your voice too. I just discovered that you attended one of our city council meetings, last June, and didn't come up and say hello." Put the son of a bitch on the defensive.

"City council, last June, huh? I can't quite . . . Oh, yes, I see it in my date book. We must keep track of these things, you know, in case we ever have to prove we've been somewhere, have an alibi if someone is murdered."

Maggie stifled a gasp in response to the word, "murdered." Why had that word popped up in his mind? Some joke!

She made an attempt at a small laugh, out of courtesy. "I was just wondering," she said, "what you thought about the meeting and whether I could fill you and the Speaker in on anything that may have been of interest?" Good, that was as leading a question as she could assemble on short notice.

"Actually, now I remember. I was in town for meetings. My hotel room was at the airport. Steven suggested I go see you in action. There's a rumor you're thinking of running for State Senate. True or false?"

Edelton was a lawyer too, she knew, so she should be careful not to give a straight yes or no answer. A straight answer would indicate she was too much of a newbie or delusional.

"I've heard those rumors too. I haven't ruled it out, but I haven't made up my mind. Still testing the waters." She couldn't help feeling pleased that anyone in the upper stratosphere of politics was at all interested in her political career. If it was true.

"I know what you mean. You need more information before you can decide. I have a pollster who has done a good job in other campaigns. I'll have my secretary provide you with his name. But let me ask you, are you sure you have the financial resources to run?"

"Money shouldn't be a problem. You know, I've got family resources and have built up a good contributor base." She was telling him what he most wanted to hear. Personal fortune always was helpful in gathering contributions because money attracts money.

"Great. I think you should get all your ducks in a row. I know the election isn't for three more years but, I have to tell you, the current state senator isn't well."

News indeed. The current State Senator was elderly, but, so far as any outsider knew, he intended to complete his term. Her heart began to thump. If he died, she could be appointed and begin to serve, which would give her a big advantage over any other candidate in the following general election.

Or was she getting the royal treatment to discourage her from asking more questions? Maggie was just as egotistical as the next politician, but didn't think she was an ideal candidate for State Senator. Was the Speaker's aide pledging some kind of support for her future in office? Too good to be true?

48

She attempted to calm herself down. "Interesting. About your pollster. I could probably use him about now."

"I'm glad to hear it. I hope we can talk again on this subject, very soon. Maybe I could suggest a political operative to run your campaign? He could give you some insight into whether to run and could be your campaign manager if you do decide to run."

She was only human, her head began to swim.

She brought herself back to reality.

I've been completely co-opted and thrown off the track, Maggie thought. If someone wanted to avoid mention of Matalokus, this was certainly the way to do that.

Was the Matalokus situation something that scared, or let's say, concerned a powerful member of her political party, so much that he'd bribe her with dreams of an office, just to shut her up? If so, why?

Chapter Nine

"Bad," Fire Chief Duego said.

"Um, sorry, I'm still asleep. Could you repeat what you said at first? What's bad?" Maggie sat up in her bed, her cell phone pushed hard against her ear. In a King-size bed, she looked lost in the covers. She should have downsized after her husband died, but couldn't bring herself to do that. This was the bed where she and her late husband created her remarkably beautiful babies.

"The fire. The strip mall that was to be torn down anyway for that project, but which never happened." She could hear sirens in the distance. "We had to call in some extra equipment from other suburbs." He coughed, possibly for effect. "Lots of smoke."

"Where are you exactly? I'm coming over."

"No need. I'm sure we'll have this under control in a few . . . soon. I'm across the street in a field. The fire is far enough away from the closest subdivision, I don't think it will spread. It's not that windy." Longer pause: "Hopefully."

Spreading fire hadn't occurred to her and certainly chased away any remnants of sleep. "Is . . . anyone inside?"

No response, but a muffling, probably the chief's attempt to cover the speaker on his cell phone and to yell at someone, without being heard by the Mayor.

Duego was a very experienced chief, had risen from the ranks and was, Maggie knew, a very brave man. His hair was getting white, but when he put on his helmet to stand for pictures with his men and women firefighters, he was still an impressive figure.

Back talking directly, Duego said, "We don't know if anyone is inside. It's 2 in the morning. I don't know why anyone would be in there, but I suppose it's possible. I don't think a strip mall of this size would have a full-time guard. Perhaps someone who checked on multiple sites in the area, one by one."

"Any cars in the parking lot?"

"Not in front, which is good, because I don't have to drag them out." Maggie, in her mind's eye, could imagine Duego lifting cars onto his back.

"I'll be there in 15 minutes. See you then."

Maggie parked along the field across the street. She could actually feel the heat. Sooty smoke came through flares of fire that reached high into the night in impromptu forms, nature's architecture. The flames reminded her of the cathedral she'd seen in Barcelona on her honeymoon, formless, without corners, but still rising to the sky.

Offhand, she couldn't remember how old the strip mall was, but weren't they usually built so there was concrete blocks between each unit? So the fire couldn't easily spread? Apparently not, or the fire was hot enough to melt bricks. Nothing had stopped the fire from engulfing the entire elongated building.

When had the city required sprinkler systems, and was this strip mall grandfathered in, so sprinklers weren't required? She had a dim memory of something in the project proposal. A promise that the project's new buildings would be much more fire resistant than the existing ones.

Several hook and ladder trucks and snorkel units were on the scene. As she watched, another large fire truck pulled in noisily close-by.

She found Duego, shouting orders, his face smudged. The odor of burning building materials hit her, acrid. She recalled a neighbor who had a fire in her utility room when lint from the clothes dryer ignited. Even though the fire was put out without too much damage, the burn smell made the house uninhabitable.

This strip mall would never reopen.

Lights were focused on the shell. Three snorkels spouts were aimed into the structure, the white water shooting through the air from above the roof. Hard to believe, she thought, that the fire could still be out of control.

As she watched, part of the roof collapsed, falling into building, like an implosion.

"There's some evidence on the surveillance tapes," Duego said abruptly. "Usually those recorders are within the building, but apparently these were on some kind of remote to the security company."

"So you thinking it was arson? A person can be identified?"

"Yes, arson. No, the arsonist had a hat almost down to his nose. We might be able to identify his lips if we ever find him.

"Did they see him come out again?"

"No, he must have monkeyed with the cameras. The recording went black. Maybe the arsonist escaped. Also we don't know if someone else was in the building. Came in during working hours or through an unsurveiled front entry after closing time. We don't know.

Duego was telling her everything he didn't know. "What about police reports? Has anyone called in saying their spouse is missing?"

"No, but it's really still too early. Some spouses aren't there when you reach out in the middle of the night. Sometimes, it's better not to know where your spouse is."

What in the world were they talking about now? Had Duego some marital problems? Maggie had met his wife and she was lovely. A good mother, a strong person. She'd be mighty upset if some day Duego perished in the flames and didn't come home to lay next to her.

The fire finally began to die down. Probably, Maggie thought, because the strip mall was almost totally consumed. If anyone was inside, he or she could not have survived. They wouldn't know anything more about the possible victims or what kind of accelerant was used to set off the blaze until morning, when the experts could sift the rubble.

She doubted that they would ever know the whole story or the motive. Maggie was well aware that store owners sometimes torch a failing business to get the insurance. Chicago was famous for more fires than just the Great Chicago Fire of 1871. The arsonist might have been a professional who was hired to do the job.

Sleep returned with images of hellish fires, souls burning for their sins. She tossed and turned, got up to get a glass a water, and, finally, ate a very early breakfast, hoping a full stomach would settle her nerves enough to let her sleep.

Duego had promised to call, even if it was still very early, to tell her when they knew more about the fire and possible victims. Dawn would come early. Perhaps enlightenment would arrive as soon as the light?

Her cell rang.

She'd forgotten to replace it near her bed, on the small table with the digital alarm clock, when she'd returned from the fire. Where had she left her purse, with the phone in it? She'd absently flung the purse away as she walked through her front door. Where was it now? Certainly not on the shelf where she put the mail before she had time to read it.

Her purse with the phone in it had fallen from the couch and Maggie had to bend to retrieve it.

She heard a familiar voice when she hit the receive button. "Maggie, it's Louise. Suzanne said you wanted to talk to me."

"I wanted to talk to you because you wanted to talk to me. What's up with you? Why are you calling so early?"

"Oh, you know, it's an hour later here," Louise said. "Why did I call you to begin with? I haven't a clue, just had a premonition you'd like to talk."

"We're having a bit of excitement here. That strip mall burned down, the one that was going to be torn down for a project."

53

"So that really was kind of fortuitous?"

She hadn't thought of that, amid all the excitement. "That's one way to look at it. I want to hear what you've been . . ."

Call waiting interrupted the conversation. The mechanical voice said "Fire Station," in Maggie's ear. "I'm really embarrassed," she said, "but it's probably the Fire Chief. I've got to talk to him. Maybe we should correspond through e-mails?"

"Fine." Louise sounded a tad insulted, but Maggie knew that she would force herself to understand that Maggie was a busy person and forgive her.

She switched to the other line. "Chief?"

"Yeah, it's me."

"What happened after I went home?"

"Mostly, we waited for the husk to cool. We had our arson expert come in, woke him up, so he could take a look around, while the crime scene was still intact. If you call floating in water intact."

"What did your expert think?"

"The fire probably started in the backroom of the restaurant. Could have been set up to look like a grease fire. There's always a lot of grease near these fryers, of course, for french fries. The man seen in the surveillance tapes wasn't carrying anything in his hands that could be seen, so he must have used the materials at hand. Once the grease flamed up higher, it must have gone into the ceiling and then spread to the other stores."

He paused to gather his thoughts. "We're not talking fireproof construction here. The strip mall had been divided and redivided or individual stores expanded with upticks in business. Whatever was between the walls to block fires had been cut through several times. I'm going to talk to the building inspectors on this one."

Good, Maggie thought. Get on it. Only you can prevent strip-mall fires, Smokey. "But was any body found?"

"We think so. Not much left. You know bones do burn if the temperature gets high enough. That's how

54

they get the ashes to go into those little memorial bottles they give to families to throw to the winds instead of burial."

"You think one body? Could it have been the arsonist?"

"I don't think so. What remained of the victim's clothes doesn't looks like what the arsonist was wearing.

Chapter Ten

Feeling embattled, Maggie, at her city hall desk, searched the front page of the local newspaper for some good news, but only saw photos of the burning strip mall and speculation about the identity of the incinerated victim.

If any effort had been made to stifle coverage until the family of the victim was notified, it had not succeeded. The local media must have found out about the death as soon as, or sooner than Maggie.

She looked up the column to the byline on the fire story: Becky Frangelmore. That explained why the article was so thorough. Becky could outferret a ferret.

Maggie was on her second cup of coffee, which was having only the minimal desired effect. Nothing made up for her lack of sleep the previous night. Her phone rang. "Maggie, it's Becky. Any word yet from the County coroner's office establishing the identity of who we don't know who?"

Littlemayor had to laugh. "If I knew who, we wouldn't need a coroner. You might have more luck with Chief Feather."

"Feather thinks I'm a feather-head. I've got to get information before detectives are officially assigned. You know, once that happens, I have to drop my coverage and another reporter has to take over."

Maggie understood. Becky wasn't allowed to cover police matters because of her husband's job as a Brunswik police detective. Berringer. Partner to Smith. Which reminded her, had Smith made any progress on learning anything about Matalokus? Was the disappearance of Matalokus somehow connected to the fire?

Maggie: "I understand. If I knew anything more, I would tell you. But let me ask you something. Is there any good news? Is anything good happening in town? I'll settle for good news anywhere on the North Shore."

Becky laughed. "Good news isn't news. The world is supposed to work. It's when it doesn't work that it's news."

The ways of the world are mysterious. "I should be doing my share of the world's work," Maggie said. She really needed to catch up with her legal practice. No court was planned for this morning, so she'd hoped for several hours of undisturbed effort.

Persisting. "One thing I don't understand," Becky said, "or should I say among the things I don't understand is why there was so little security within the restaurant. Why we don't know anything after the arsonist entered the property."

She could share a little. "I thought about the same thing," Maggie said. "The way it was explained to me this morning by the Chief Duego, who talked to the security company, is that the restaurant had an internal surveillance camera but it was only focused on the cash register. We aren't talking about a franchise restaurant or a four-star. This was a mostly take-out place with a few tables. If someone was careful, he'd be able to avoid the camera inside altogether."

"Ha!" Becky's curiosity satisfied and certainly having enough new information for a follow up story, she, nevertheless, asked, "How long do you think it'll take before the autopsy is in?"

"I don't know. I saw on the Internet that murders are down. No records broken in Chicago this year, but it's still early."

"So you think our body might get an early . . .examination, inspection, touching, probing, whatever they do in an autopsy?"

"I don't know." With a twinge, she thought, the only people looking at my body, are my doctors, and I have to pay them to do that. Changing the subject in her

57

own mind, she asked, "Why do you think someone wanted to burn down the strip mall?"

"I think someone is getting impatient for the project to proceed." So Becky felt, like Louise, that, in a sense, someone tried to speed up, encourage, push for the completion of the mall project by burning down the present mall. Interesting. Becky went on: "I don't think it's one of the store owners who burnt strip mall down. That wouldn't make a lot of sense. These businesses are in the trash now until something happens to build another mall."

Interviewing a reporter for fun and profit. "What about the dead man? Who do you think he was?"

"I think it was the arsonist. He started the fire then was hoist by his own petard."

"Good for you!" Maggie said. "I haven't heard that phrase since college. Congratulations on working that into a conversation!"

"It's nothing for a wordsmith," Becky said. Still not out of questions, she asked, "Do you think this was a professional arson?"

"His ability to hide his face and to knock out the camera in the back seems to indicate that. Uh-oh, did I reveal something that you didn't know? Please don't quote me on that. I'm not an expert, just giving my impression."

"Weren't there cameras in front of the strip mall?" Becky asked.

"I wondered the same thing. But, you know, this was an old mall, small. I don't think the store owners were terribly worried about someone breaking in the front. Police come around regularly, as does the guard from the security company. I'm just guessing here. I think the business owners only worried was that someone would bring a truck around the back and empty an entire inventory."

"Speculation at its finest. You'll be reading about it in the newspaper and on the Internet."

Back in her law office, an unexpected call interrupted her editing of a complaint. "Hello, Ma!" Both the voice and the manner of greeting told Maggie who was calling. Tracy, the daughter who wasn't feuding with her for no known reason, the older of her two daughters. How amazingly different the two were in personality and disposition!

"Tracy, how nice to hear your voice. Where are you?" Tracy did a considerable amount of traveling. She was moving up the corporate ladder as an executive for a large international company that shipped food for other large international companies. At least, Maggie thought that's what it did. Maybe not.

"I'm in town, just until Saturday. I'll be busy with meetings until Friday night, but I want to arrange to have dinner with you." Dramatic pause. "And there's a handsome young man I want you to meet."

This could only mean the long awaited, prayed for, serious relationship was here at last. Maggie had a sudden urge to cry. Her beautiful daughter, close to 35 years old, still hadn't settled down to have a family. Maggie had read all the articles about how career women missed out on what Maggie considered the essentials in life: love, home, and children.

Kimberly, the younger sister, had chosen the opposite extreme, the more traditional lifestyle, home and family but no career. She only used her degree to do part-time teaching, so she could be home for her own children after school. Maggie approved, up to a point, but hoped Kimberly would do more with her life, as she, herself, had done.

Was this the problem? Was Kimberly mad at me, Maggie wondered, because I also wanted a career, as well as a family? Did I neglect her while I was doing my legal work? People always say the younger child is ignored.

No, that wasn't the problem, Maggie decided. She knew in her heart that she had never stinted on Kimberly in any way or treated her older daughter better. Maggie truly believed she'd given Kimberly as much attention and love as Tracy.

Hadn't she?

Get back on track.

"I'm so happy to hear from you, and this is interesting news about a young man." She didn't want to jinx the situation by making too much about being introduced to a potential mate for her daughter. Hopefully, someone as special as her daughter, herself.

"Let's meet over at Andretti's at 7:30 Friday night," Tracy said. "How does that sound?"

"Great, you've made my whole week. I really needed something to look forward to."

"Is there a city crisis? Are they overworking you as mayor?" This was a common theme in their conversations. Tracy thought Maggie worked much too hard for a woman of her... age? Vintage? Senility?

"Just the ordinary aggravations plus a few challenges that must be overcome. Nothing that will prevent me from meeting you for dinner. How's your career going?"

A short hesitation. "One always hopes for smoother sailing."

Doesn't one? Maggie sure did. "Do you want me to make the reservations? I always get treated well and I'm given a table in front so everyone can see the Mayor."

"No. I'll do it. I don't want us to be interrupted by your constituents and complainers while we eat."

Maggie felt the afterglow of talking to her wonderful daughter. She couldn't wait to hear the details if, as she hoped, Tracy was engaged.

Turning back to her work, she found concentration difficult. She berated herself. She thought, I should be excited at the idea of getting some justice for my client. So what if I've done this a million times before.

A call from Detective Smith shook her out of her reverie. "Yes, hello, detective, have you learned something about the Matalokus family?" Before he could answer, she provided him with the one bit of information she'd gathered herself. "I found out that Severn had a wife at the June meeting. I thought that he was a widower."

She remembered distinctly that Severn said he was a widower. Perhaps he thought being single would help him to win her approval for his project? That he could influence her that way? As if all women are constantly looking for a man and lose their wits as soon as they find out a man is single. A bit of chauvinism, anti-feminism?

Smith said, "No, I hadn't heard that. I haven't researched every possible digital police source yet, but I'm not finding anything about the Matalokus clan, other than about the death of his brother. You knew about that, right?"

"Yes." She felt a little guilty about withholding that information as a test of Smith's research ability. "Did you find out anything about the murder investigation afterwards?"

"Just the usual busy work until the matter is dropped. No speculation about why Anthony was killed. I have nothing else about the Matalokus clan. Either they had unreachable juvenile records or are otherwise very dull. Not even traffic or parking tickets."

What, did all the Matalokuses ride around in limousines from birth? No tickets even for speeding or jaywalking? Severn didn't seem like the altogether harmless type. He was an adventurer, for sure. A land pirate.

"But," Smith said," I have an appointment to talk to someone in Highplace, a relative on the police force who might be helpful. I'll get back to you on that. To change the subject, I suppose you've heard the bad news."

A sinking feeling. No, and why am I the last to know? I hate that. "What?"

"You will find this very disturbing. Don't say you got it from me, but the preliminary findings are that the victim of the strip mall fire is someone you know."

Uh-oh, she thought, I'm getting the treatment where information is dribbled out, so I don't have a collapse when I get the whole story. Don't tell me right away that my dog is dead; start by telling me my dog is ill and work up to its death.

"Alderman Casey. Identified by some charred identification. And his wife finally called in a missing person report."

Shock and regret.

Alderman Casey, her rival, either as a successor for the mayoral job or for the State Senate position, was dead. The discussion of her political future as a State Senator with   Edelton and the indicated support of O'Malley, probably the most powerful politician in the state, had been followed in a few hours, not days, by the death of Casey. Eliminating her competitor.

Wasn't this too closely linked to be coincidental?

Horrible thought: Was Casey killed to help my political career? Was Casey dead because of me?

Chapter Eleven

Under the byline of Becky Frangelmore:

A Brunswik alderman perished early Wednesday morning in a strip-mall fire at Third and Main streets, an apparent victim of arson.

Gene Casey, 44, a life-long resident of the Fourth Ward and its alderman for the last 7 years was identified by a credit card which had not completely melted during the conflagration, according to police sources.

A full autopsy is expected to be completed within a week, according to an Assistant Cook County Coroner. It is not known whether Casey was killed by the fire, or whether the fire was created to cover up his murder.

No other victim of the fire has been found or identified.

Police believe the fire was arson, because a furtive person, whose face was mostly covered by a hoodie and who has not been identified, entered the strip-mall, into the Paisley Pump Restaurant, 1061 Third Avenue, at around 1:30 a.m., after disabling a surveillance camera in the rear of the mall.

The arsonist apparently started a fire utilizing the materials in the building, especially grease for frying food.

The arsonist, based on the recorded entrance and comparative measurements, was too short to be the alderman, who was 6 feet tall, police sources reported. Moreover, the body found was wearing a suit known to resemble one owned by Casey, not a hoodie.

No reason for Casey's presence in the restaurant at night has been established.

Police speculate that Casey was either in the building at closing time or somehow gained entrance from the front of the shopping mall. Surveillance cameras were not directed towards the front, street side, of the shopping mall, which consists of other stores besides the restaurant.

As far as is known, Casey had no connection to the restaurant, financial or otherwise, except as a very infrequent patron. An autographed photo of Casey with the current owner hung near the cash register at the front of the restaurant, according to other patrons, along with about a dozen other photos of local and state politicians and sports figures.

Casey was a well-known and successful lawyer, specializing in real estate transfers and foreclosures. His firm, Casey, Benedict, and Mason was established by Casey's father in the 1950's. Casey was chairman of the Real Estate Committee of the city council and worked closely with the city's Planning Commission. He also served on the Board of Directors for the Timming Bank on Central, and was active in coaching a junior basketball team.

The Council approved a Planning Commission recommendation in June to tear down the strip mall where Casey ultimately perished and replace it with a department store and other storefronts. The proposed parking lot would include surrounding lots not presently developed.

The project was proposed by Severn Matalokus, a real estate developer, but has apparently stalled. No reason for the delay into the spring has been publicly announced.

Brunswik Mayor Maggie Wellington praised Alderman Casey as a hard-working and dedicated public servant, who had a bright future in politics. "His steady hand will be greatly missed by the city council and the city's sympathy and support is extended to his family in this time of need."

Casey is survived by a widow and two children. No date for the late alderman's funeral has been announced, pending the autopsy report and release of his body to his family. A family spokesman advised that charitable contributions can be made in his honor into a scholarship fund, which will be established in his name.

Casey had been mentioned both as a mayoral and as a State Senatorial candidate.

State law allows the appointment of an alderman by the Mayor, with the consent of the council, to complete the final year of Casey's term in office.

When would she receive her first phone call from someone who wanted to succeed Casey and who would it be?

Maggie sat in her office in city hall and reread Becky's article. The quote attributed to her was only approximate and was a little more grammatical than the original. A good reporter doesn't, won't let a good source sound like an idiot.

Would the potential candidates wait for a respectable time or would they begin their candidacy dance even before Casey was lowered into his grave? Dancing on the promise of a grave?

Her phone rang. She saw the name on the readout. She should have known. Rauptt was also a resident of the Fourth Ward, as had been Casey, residency being a requirement to be the alderman.

Would Rauptt begin by expressing his deep sorrow about the death of Casey, then ease into questions about his replacement, then finally suggest that, if it was in the best interest of the city, he, Rauptt, might take up the burden?

"Hello, dear lady, it's Edgar." Maggie was a little surprised that he used his first name, since everyone always called him just Rauptt, sometimes adding a syllable, as in "Raup-tuh." She'd almost forgotten his first name.

"I just wanted to call to express my deep sorrow regarding the death of Alderman Casey, a man with whom I'd worked many hours and whom I came to know and like. He was my junior in age, but I felt he was my mentor in the city administration. I learned a lot from him. I was like his disciple, but he never failed to compliment me on my own knowledge and expertise. He will be greatly missed. The city has lost one of its pillars, one of its giants."

Stopping just short of saying, as was said about Lincoln, that he "now belongs to the ages."

"I know, I know," Maggie said. I know which way the wind doth blow. Alright, enough, give me your best pitch!

Rauptt began. "During this interim period while we learn to live without Alderman Casey's wise stewardship, I can only express my willingness to assume whatever responsibilities the city and you, dear lady, wish to ask of me. I feel I can rise to the occasion."

Use of the word "rise," suggested both an erection and dough to Maggie, but, in Rauptt's case, mostly dough.

Rauptt would make a lousy alderman. He didn't like people. He certainly wasn't a pat-you-on-the-back kind of guy. Hello, nice to see you, how's the family? How's the little guy with the peg leg, still stumping around? Are you still beating your wife?

On the other hand, Rauptt was a known, whereas anyone new might be a crazed person with a personal agenda to destroy the city. Such people existed. Not wild eyed or easily identifiable before gaining office. Only later did such a person feel he had been anointed, not just elected, and all the crazy things he'd said to himself were actually not delusions. Most disturbingly, he would take himself utterly seriously, start seeing conspiracies everywhere, and become paranoid until everyone was completely against him.

Rauptt could at least be trusted to be Rauptt. A drudge who got things done. So why not? "I wonder, Edgar, if you would consider ever taking to role in the theater of politics? After all, appointment would give you a head start over other candidates next year."

Was it possible to actually feel, through a cell phone, the sucking up of air as someone expands his ego to the bursting point? "Oh, dear lady, I can't believe that you would suggest that. I feel so honored to even be considered for the appointment. I'm a little choked up."

Me too, Maggie thought, but for me it's more like gagging. "I wonder, while you are considering this step that will change your life, if I can ask you something?"

"If you're asking whether there is anything in my background that would prevent me from being a fine alderman, I'm happy to tell you my record is spotless."

Without "spot"? He never had a dog named Spot? "I'm sure," Maggie said, somewhat distracted from her intent. "Perhaps you could write out a statement of your background and expertise, a resume of sorts, so that I can have some talking points when the council asks me for my recommendation."

"Of course, of course." Doubtlessly, he was already creating a mental list of his qualifications and experience. Were you elected to clean the chalkboards in the third grade? Don't forget that course in political science in college.

She'd try again to change the subject away from his ego-gratification. "I wonder, as long as we're talking like this. Open and honest," Maggie said, "If you had any idea why Casey was in that restaurant prior to the tragedy?"

"I cannot imagine."

"He never mentioned anything about the restaurant to you?"

"Just in passing, when we were considering where the businesses in the strip mall might migrate into the new buildings. His interest in the restaurant was no more or less than in any other business. We did meet once with all the current owners, who were very enthusiastic. I have just a dim memory of the restaurant owner. A Greek." Mentioning ethnicity must have suddenly reminded him to whom he was talking. Uh-oh. Isn't Littlemayor a Greek? "Of course, a very fine man. Very good reputation in the community. A fine family man, I'm sure."

Good save.

Maggie had a sudden thought that of all who might be involved in the project, Rauptt might be the one who would most benefit from Casey's death. Other than herself.

Chapter Twelve

"Mr. Wally has received your name from the Speaker and wonders if you might come downtown to discuss your possible upcoming campaign?"

A very careful and formal woman was on the cell. Much as Maggie would be if she'd been forced to contact a lunatic, someone crazy enough to actually want to run for office. Afraid to say anything that might set the poor fool off, disturb the equanimity established through medication.

She was in her law office. "I see. Yes, I would like to talk to Mr. Wally." Drop some names. "Mr. Edelton, the Speaker's aide, said a political operative would contact me about possibly running, so I suppose this is in regard to that?" Asking for a clarification might be a sign of sanity. Let's hope.

Not answering questions today, thank you. "Mr. Wally will be available at 1 p.m. today. I'm afraid he is traveling shortly after that. You know, meeting with officials and candidates downstate. Really the best time is today. Is that possible for you?"

Maggie dreaded driving downtown. She wasn't xenophobic about the big city, just knew to avoid the crush of cars, the aggravation of finding a place to park, the self-absorbed crowds and the panhandlers on the street, who saddened her.

"Of course, if that's all the available time he has. Perhaps he is too busy to help me?" See if this is a bit of a pose. The important man too busy to see the idiot candidate. Get him while you can, or else he'll go and run someone else into the ground.

Ignoring her question, the administrative assistant said, "Splendid. I'll pencil you in. We're in the Wellington building at State and Madison. Oh, isn't that a coincidence, Mayor Wellington? Are you a Wellington, like the Wellington who built this sky scrapper?"

"Wellington is my married name." At least give me the respect normally granted to any married woman. That someone loved me so much he wanted to be my husband.

The administrative assistant decided to be distracted, rather than be drawn into a discussion of her own marital history. "We'll look forward to seeing you then. That's suite 1014, if I haven't mentioned it yet."

She broke the connection.

No reason to make the trip downtown as unpleasant as possible. Who could she get to accompany her or even drive instead of her? Much more pleasant to spend the time socializing.

She decided to ask Harper. A good idea. An entourage of even one would make her look more credible, more like a real, happening candidate. Someone there with a clip board, making sure that the candidate was on time for her next important speaking engagement. Like in the movies.

She walked over to Harper's alcove. Her desk was piled high with papers, but not in a messy or disorganized way, and she was typing rapidly on a keyboard. The computer screen was reflected in her glasses.

Maggie told her of the need to go downtown to meet the political operative and that she could use some company.

Harper waved at the papers on her desk. "If you think I can spare the time, I wouldn't mind going. Maybe I'd learn something about the lives of politicians. Not that I want such a life, no insult meant or intended."

"None received. Think of this as part of your education. See the political creatures in their natural habitat."

Harper drove, which was a blessing. Each time she was on the expressways, Maggie had to relearn how to drive in intense traffic.

How much better it is, she thought, to live close to one's job. A long daily commute must subtract years from the life of the commuter. And Brunswik is considered one of the closer, inner suburbs. She could only imagine how awful it would be to drive on a daily basis from the state line with Wisconsin to downtown.

Harper was quiet, concentrating on her driving, but began to relax when they reached a spot on the expressway, after the toll booths, where traffic eased somewhat. It was mid-day after all. The morning rush hour was long over and the evening rush was hours away. Things wouldn't pick up until after 3 p.m. when the schools let out and teachers began to drive home.

"How are you, dear?" Maggie asked Harper. "Sorry, I'm so wrapped up in myself, I hardly have time to notice anyone around me. What's the latest on the dating front? Are you still going with that cute guy you met at a party? The one you described as a 'hunk, dreamboat, stud.'"

"The dreamboat part was half right. He turned out to be a dream, as in a nightmare. Two dates and I'd had enough of his egocentricity. It was like I wasn't there. He talked about himself the whole time. Asked me two questions on the second date, and the second question was 'how about sleeping with me?'"

"Things haven't changed so much since my dating days, obviously. But, don't stop trying. There is a man out there for you."

"Is the effort worth it?"

"Yes. There are good men out there, despite what the media says and the villains in movies. Good guys, sweet, who want to love you back, as best they can. Loyal, steady, smart, caring. Yes, aggravating, impossible, unable to express themselves, but kind and oh so funny. While living with one, you don't know how you survive, and then, when he's gone, you miss him so much, you can't remember that he only listened with half a brain, that it never occurred to him to pick something up. Gone and there's a big hole in your life."

71

"You really miss the late Mr. Wellington, don't you? I'm sorry. I can't imagine being a widow. I'm still trying to imagine being a wife."

"Good things will come to you if you keep your self-respect. Really, a good man is waiting out there for you."

"I earnestly hope you are right. Should I carry a sign, 'Good man, I'm here.'"

"In a way."

When they found Mr. Wally's suite, the door was open, but no one sat at the front desk and the inner office door was shut.

Perhaps the receptionist and Mr. Wally were still at lunch? Or had some state political crisis beckoned and Mr. Wally was forced to leave so abruptly that no call had been made to cancel her appointment?

She didn't think she was so insignificant a politician that she could be totally ignored without an explanation.

Maybe she really was insignificant? Let's be honest, she thought. I have all the power and authority of a political hack from a small suburb. Insulting me will not create a tsunami that will sink the ship of state or even cause a ripple on a placid sea.

Maggie heard sounds within the inner sanctum of what must be Mr. Wally's office. So Mr. Wally was in. Perhaps the receptionist/administrative assistant was being lectured on the proper respect to be shown all prospective clients? That would be fitting.

No, that can't be it. If Wally was in, the only reasonable excuse for ignoring the appointment would be that Wally was too busy with some complex political maneuver, trying to save the day and someone's campaign.

But it wasn't even an election year.

Maggie looked at Harper. Would the young woman become cynical in the ways of the world if Maggie was treated with disrespect? Harper didn't look abashed by the discourtesy. She was smiling and rolling her eyes.

Obviously, Harper's sharper hearing had discerned something that Maggie's had missed. Her hearing was good for her age, but she would never claim to have the same acute audial sense she had in her early 20's. Too many loud rock concerts when she was young, too many airplanes. Her mother had been somewhat deaf towards the end of her life, and maybe Maggie would succumb to the same. On the brighter side, they did wonders with hearing aides these days.

Maggie listened more intently. These were not the angry tones of a lecture to one's subordinate or the profundities doled out by a political guru to his disciple.

No, these were the rhythmic sounds of an approaching crisis of some sort. Dare she think the word "Orgasm"?

More writhing behind he door, then silence, followed by soft murmurings. Where had the intimacy taken place, exactly? On the desk? That seemed like a very uncomfortable surface, not conducive to passionate exchange.

The receptionist/administrative assistant/passion partner opened the door a crack and gazed out. Maggie caught a glimpse of a chagrined face. Also, Mr. Wally must have a very rough beard because the woman's fair-skinned cheeks glowed from contact burns.

The door shut again, and after a pause, surely for the purpose of composing herself and straightening her clothes, the woman emerged. She had a neon-bright, profound blush.

No explanation or apology was provided.

"Mr. Wally will see you now."

Chapter Thirteen

She and Harper sat in front of Mr. Wally's desk. Maggie was afraid to look at the desktop and moved her eyes around the room, hoping to see a different venue for the love-making.

Thank goodness, Maggie thought, there is a large couch.

Preliminaries completed, Mr. Wally launched into what Maggie guessed was his usual introductory lecture. Maggie listened as best she could, but Mr. Wally talked much too fast. She could only latch onto a few key words. That, however, was sufficient.

Mr. Wally was a small man, slim, about 40 and beginning to gray, with a merciless, apparently near-lethal 5 o'clock shadow.

If Maggie had to choose an animal most like Mr. Wally, she would have chosen a mongoose. Quick, feral, he had no compunction about using any tactic to gain the advantage. Like his totem animal, Mr. Wally would seize the neck of any political cobra and shake it until his sharp little teeth separated the head from the body.

The main thing was the election, to be elected, getting elected was everything, he emphasized. Challenge the signatures on the nominating petitions, allege lack of residence, impugn marital harmony, dig up sexual history, if necessary. Anything to reach the magical, life-changing status of being elected.

Maggie was not surprised to hear that Mr. Wally didn't distinguish between political parties on the basis of philosophy or ideals. In fact, he'd represented almost as many Republicans as Democrats. She sincerely doubted that he held any firm political position on any issue.

Principles weren't necessary. Not my job, he said. I'm a political hired gun.

Maggie had met this type before. And scrupulously avoided them. In her own campaigns, she'd relied on some fine people to get out the vote, unpaid volunteers who wanted to elect her because of her personal and political ideals.

Mr. Wally was the opposite. He would help you or anyone for a fee. On the other hand, he thought this was a kind of integrity. Integrity of a sort. Once his loyalty was bought, he emphasized, it was inviolate.

Mr. Wally cradled his fingers and pushed back in his chair. Aggressively. He was a very aggressive man. Nothing wrong with that. Nobody likes the namby-pamby. He was just a thug, but sometimes, apparently, you just need a thug. Mr. Not-Nice so the candidate could maintain a somewhat nice, at least nonbelligerent, image.

"I've handled many state senatorial races. You know Senators" X, Y, and Z? She recalled their names and could even picture the face of one, but couldn't for the life of her remember anything they'd accomplished in office.

She was lucky, Mr. Wally insisted, because Mr. Wally was excellent, superior in his job. He had all the important connections. He was Best Friends Forever with Speaker O'Malley, often played golf with the former governor, went to all of the political elite's Christenings, Bar Mitvahs, debutante rituals, and weddings. His friends would immediately become her friends.

"I know the inside story on everyone," he said. "The truth behind the facade. I am in constant touch with other political operatives and constantly having lunch with the politicians who make the actual decisions."

She wondered if Mr. Wally would someday use her name in vanity when talking to other politicians. As in, "Maggie Wellington didn't have a chance in hell but I put her on the right path. She placed her political future in my hands, and I ran with the ball."

"I'm not sure exactly what a political operative does, if you don't mind me asking?"

"Everything," he said, "everything necessary to get a candidate elected. From soup to nuts."

Maggie was sure about the nuts part, as in insane.

"My job begins with creating an image for the candidate that will, surefire, get him elected. Some characteristic, true or not, that the voters can grab ahold of, to humanize him or her. A hobby, a personal struggle to overcome great odds, a love of family, like that. Once my client is elected, my job ends and he or she can go back to his real personality until the next political cycle."

Maggie felt overwhelmed. Wait! "I'm a person with definite ideas," she explained.

"Better to keep them to yourself. Political positions ruffles feathers. But if you must, write down your political views on a yellow legal pad and I will keep them in your folder if I ever need to refer to them. Try to remember, the person is elected who most makes the voter believe he is voting for himself. Every foray into an issue may cost you more than you gain."

If you are so darn smart, "What do you see as my chances for election?"

This put Mr. Wally in a contemplative mode. He made the appearance of dredging up, from the depths of his soul, some wisdom to impart. "I see you as having a very good chance, a very good chance, indeed. I've surveyed the field of candidates, and done some preliminary spadework."

That makes it sound, Maggie thought, like he is digging a grave. Mine.

"The incumbent has decided--this is not for current publication, of course--that he will not run. If the proper foundation is poured, you have an excellent chance." Both a gravedigger and a cement mixer, she thought. "No other Democrat is strong enough to take the job from you, now that Alderman Casey is dead."

He paused and gave her a meaningful look, as if asking whether she'd killed him.

Maggie felt very uncomfortable and even a little guilty, as if gaining an advantage from Alderman Casey's murder implicated her in some way.

When she didn't admit to personally burning Casey to cinders, Mr. Wally continued. "A wonderful advantage." Mr. Wally is expressing glee over the death of a human being, she thought. "You'll be appointed to fill his term and won't have your date with destiny and the voters for at least another year."

How can he be so positive I'll be appointed? Mr. Wally seemed to have secret knowledge about everything. A magician privy to secret and arcane knowledge.

76

"Appointment also means, among other things, that you probably won't be facing a primary with other Democrats, and the voters will see you can handle the job, just by not getting yourself in trouble. You would have a great advantage over the probable Republican candidate, Nasheti. He's only held very local offices but is very rich. Ben Edelton says you are rich, too. Am I right?"

"Yes," Maggie said, embarrassed to be saying something out loud, in front of Harper, that her own mother always said was gauche and only to be discussed in private.

You have answered the question correctly! Mr. Wally approves and is giving you a big smile, lips open, showing his little mongoose teeth. "You need to nail down some support before you announce your candidacy, of course. Also, we'll need to begin the polling which will show you are the peoples' choice."

Surprise must have shown on her face and some skepticism. "You already know what the polls will show?"

"I know this because women always poll well at this level and your name is not totally unknown. We know who's voting and most of their preferences, block by block, residence by residence. We have computer programs that keep track. Besides, the poll will be weighted for Brunswik and the immediate surrounding areas. Before the telephoning begins, you'll do a little public speaking on the borders of the district, which, as you know, is gerrymandered Democratic. Some favorable newspaper articles will providentially appear."

Slow down, Maggie thought. Remembering what else he had said, "Whose support do you want me to nail down?"

"Easy peezy, in my humble opinion. You need to have a long talk with the incumbent, Markham. He's got to be enthusiastic so we can co-op his organization. Secondly, you have to talk to Michaels." Who? Maggie had no idea who Michaels was. "His family has been the power in the district for generations. He's so influential no one knows who is. Lastly, I want you to talk to a banker who can deliver up contributions from the business class. Each of these people will ask for some concessions---let's call them promises---in return for their support."

Stand on my head, break the record for the three minute mile, swim the English Channel, climb the highest mountain?

"Now, before I agree to take you on, I need to know some things about you."

Wait, wasn't this interview so I could decide if I should hire you? Guess not. "What would you like to know?"

"I know you're an ethnic. That's great because Nasheti is an ethnic too. What I need to know is whether there is something in the past, something the newspapers and blogs could dredge up, that would come back to haunt you?"

"Nothing I can think of. I'm not sure exactly what you mean."

"Was your father or late husband by any chance in organized crime?"

No, and thank goodness, Maggie thought. Both were head and shoulders better men than you. "No. Honest businessmen. Spotless." Without spot.

"Really?" One "really" wasn't enough. "Really?"

About to lose her temper, finally. "Yes, really."

"How about yourself? Any legal cases pending that would put you in the news? Any lieutenants who have their fingers in the cash-box or honey pot? Have you personally got your own hands dirty in any way?"

Maggie looked at her hands. She'd done nothing . . .yet, to bring any shame upon herself. Maggie shook her head.

Mr. Wally gave her a skeptical look. "Really?"

"Yes, really." She'd never be able to talk to this man without cringing. Was it really, really a good idea to seek higher office if she must deal with people like Mr. Wally?"

78

"I'm very pleased with you as a candidate, so far." Mr. Wally said. "I think we're on the path to success."

Had she missed the portion of the interview during which she had hired Mr. Wally? He was already scheming on her behalf, assuming she would pay him whatever he asked.

She could imagine the telephone call that would follow from this meeting: she's a peach, a complete neophyte, will take any kind of advice we give her. I'm a little worried that she's not willing to admit she'd done anything wrong, but I'm pretty sure we can get away with it, if any of her scandals come to light. She, at least, looks honest.

Maggie felt like she'd been put into a food processor and the blades were beginning to spin.

"There's only one more thing," Mr. Wally said. "You've got to put a stopper on this Matalokus thing, before it bites you on the ass."

Chapter Fourteen

"I feel like I'm having a cynicism hangover," Maggie said.

Harper's eyes were on the road, driving back to Brunswik and possibly towards reality. She chanced a brief look away to see Maggie's expression, to confirm her words.

Whatever was on Maggie's face, Harper seemed reassured that the real Maggie had not yet disappeared. Harper took a deep breath. "I'm glad you said that. I was afraid you were falling for that load of crap from Mr. Wally. It's not my job to advise you, but didn't you think that was one of the weirdest experiences of your life?"

"Yes," Maggie said. "An out-of-body experience."

"I know you'd like to be a State Senator," Harper said, "but what was that all that other stuff about?"

"I wish I knew. Yes, I'd like to be a State Senator, but, no, I don't want to become a conscienceless, ruthless phony. I'm not quite ready to give up who I am."

"Good."

"The thing is though," Maggie said, "something is happening and it seems to be coalescing around me. I don't know why and I can't seem to escape it."

Harper was silent. "I really don't know what to tell you."

"Someone is missing and someone is already dead, and somehow this is my problem. It's like being sucked into someone else's life. And all I can do is watch as it unfolds and try to keep myself intact."

"Are you going to talk to the people he suggested?" Harper asked.

"I don't know."

"Matalokus' marital status can't be proven by documentation," Detective Smith said, readjusting himself in his seat in front of Maggie's mayoral desk. "He is apparently married and has a wife but I can't find any marriage records for him within the United States. If he married outside the United States, like a destination marriage in Timbuktu, I can't be as confident that there is no record, because of the problems with translation. But a search of his name worldwide only found some old, very old marriages in Greece for some Matalokuses, but not for a Severn."

"Are you suggesting some kind of a screw-up?" she asked. "Like, maybe, the courthouse with the records burned down? The judge didn't file a return on the marriage certificate or was really a used car salesman? You're not suggesting that he changed his name to Matalokus after he got married? Maybe his real original name was Wellington?"

Smith made a sad smile. "All those are possible, actually good suggestions to explain the inexplicable. Another explanation would be that somehow he was able to bribe enough people to remove his marriage from the public record. I can't imagine why someone would go to the trouble and expense, but I suppose anything is possible. Just that I've never heard of something like that happening."

Maggie pursed her lips. Had Smith missed something? Hard to believe.

He must have seen the doubt in her face. "I'm not the first one to investigate Matalokus' marital status. I know from my uncle, who is a sergeant on the Highplace Police Force and who knows all, that no one else has been able to find his marital records either."

"Well, someone signed into the Council meeting in June as his wife. She was real. The camera doesn't lie. She sat there and smiled at him from the front row."

"If he was or is married and his marriage certificate is somehow missing, he must still be married. I found no divorce papers for Severn Matalokus and no death certificate for any woman married to him."

One thing was clear. Matalokus couldn't be a widower. Why did he tell her he was? The only possible explanation: he must have felt a widower had a better chance to winning her support. She had to admit that thinking Severn had suffered as she had the loss of a mate made her more sympathetic to his mall proposals.

"On the other hand . . .," Smith said. Are five fingers, Maggie thought. ". . . the consensus is that he does or did have a wife," Smith said, "or someone who acted damn like a wife. People who worked at the Matalokus mansion in the past said there was a woman who called herself Mrs. Matalokus. Somebody named Mrs. Olivia Matalokus continued to use a debit card on a house account after Matalokus dropped out of sight. Utility bills for the mansion continued to be paid. Food is still being delivered. But no one has seen her for an unknown period and certainly not since the man himself went missing. She might still be living in the mansion. Maybe she's in the limo that goes to Matalokus Holdings every morning and returns at night."

"Or," Maggie said, "she's walled up in the mansion, like in an Edgar Allen Poe short story."

"Maybe they're both behind a wall," he said. "The detectives in Highplace have a lottery going on when, what date, they will find Matalokus and/or his wife/not wife is/are dead."

Really? "I feel like we've crossed the line into Never-Neverland," Maggie said. "It's become very important, all of sudden, to know what became of him. Like the city is frozen in place." More like I'm frozen in place until we find out what happened to him, she thought.

Smith nodded sympathetically. "Can't the city just find another developer?"

"Easier said than done, according to Rauptt, and the murder of Alderman Casey also complicates the issue." Complicates my damn issues too, she thought.

"There really isn't much else a policeman from Brunswik can do, jurisdiction-wise. Have you thought of seeking help from the FBI? Kidnapping is a federal offense."

"No, I don't want to do that, because I don't want to draw any more attention to this, whatever this is, than it already has."

"Maggie, it's Becky. Have I reached you at a bad time?"

Maggie pressed the cell phone to her ear. She was in her law office and leaned back in her chair.

How to answer? Not so upset as bewildered. "No, I have a few minutes to chat. What's up?"

"Do you want the legitimate question or the secret motive question?"

"The secret one. I'm in full secret mode today."

"You know your assistant, Harper?"

"I do. She's my paralegal. Did you want to talk to her?"

"No," Becky said, "not yet. She's second year law, right?"

"Yes, and she'll be a good lawyer if I don't ruin her for the profession."

"Well, we have a part-time reporter, a stringer, here at the paper, who's in his third year in law school. He's very nice. I like him. Harper isn't going with someone is she?"

Maggie's female radar buzzed on. The matchmaking portion of her brain began to churn. She too wanted to fix up every single man with a wife. So he could be truly happy. "Harper just ended a short and unsatisfying relationship."

"Would she like to meet our stringer? He's charming and not ugly, maybe almost cute."

A high recommendation indeed. "Sounds good. I'll walk over to Harper's desk and give her the phone."

"Great. After I've improved her life 100 per cent, I want to ask you my other question."

"What I wanted to ask," Becky said, her matchmaking complete and the cell phone returned, "was if there were any new developments in the Alderman Casey investigation?"

"I was just about to talk to Chief Feather for an update," Maggie said. "Not that I think he'll tell me anything, but maybe I can deduce something from the way he avoids telling me anything."

"Well, if anything comes out, I hope you will consider telling me. Just for background and personal gossipy curiosity. I can't actually write anything about the murder now that detectives have been assigned. Not my husband, but still, a police matter, so I'm forbidden. But I can tell you something."

"What?"

"There's to be a memorial service for Alderman Casey at First Pres this Sunday."

"You're right. That's news to me."

"You're sure to be invited. Many have already indicated that they want to say some words in eulogy. Would you want to?"

"Sure, I can force out some words, if asked. I'll have to consider what to say. I wasn't all that close to Casey but I didn't dislike him either. I like his wife. When I called with my condolences, she was very gracious, holding herself together, poor thing."

"So I can write that you'll be there."

"You can say that the Mayor's office indicated that she may attend if city business allows."

"I tell you what. I'll call the minister and tell him you're interested in being invited to speak so he can get back to you and close the loop."

"Alright. Anything else, dear?"

"I'm hearing murmurs that you are running for State Senate and I'm writing an article about it."

Maggie wavered between being pleased and being appalled that people were interested in her future plans.

What price, exactly, will I pay for my small ambition to do some good as a State Senator? "It's too early to say. You can write that I love being mayor of Brunswik and higher office is a very distant

84

consideration. That I wouldn't absolutely rule it out, if I was needed. That's a pretty innocuous statement. Who says I should run?"

"Now I have to be coy. I told him and her that I wouldn't say who, wouldn't reveal my sources."

"Fine. I'll be curious if anyone else thinks I should run, once they've read your article."

"Good, I'm already writing it in my mind."

"What did Harper say about a fix-up?"

"She wants to double with my husband and me. She said that, if I could find some nice gentleman, you could triple with us."

"Please, no, I have a full plate at the moment. My daughter's in town and I'm getting ready to meet her possibly intended. Besides, all my romances are in the past. I'm at a different stage of my life."

"I'm not listening," Becky said.

Chapter Fifteen

"Let's say, theoretically, hypothetically, that it is necessary to burglarize a house."

"Please put the sane Maggie on the phone," Louise said. "What house and why do you want to break into it?"

Maggie put her cup of tea back on the end table in her bedroom and drew her knitted coverlet up to her waist. Louise, on the other end of the telephone conversation, was in some hotel room, this time on the West Coast.

"Oh, just a random thought. Like many others. Waking from a dream with the idea that many problems could be solved if I could just do what no one else has the guts to do. Act to finally solve a mystery. Is a missing man in his house? Also, whether his wife is bricked in somewhere in the basement."

"Oh, dear," Louise said. "I'm coming home soon, and you can come to my office, throw yourself on my couch and tell me all about it. This is beginning to sound a little like a compulsion, an obsession. Like being an arsonist. Not wanting to, but feeling compelled to do the deed anyway. I certainly can write you a prescription for some medication that will cheer you right up."

"I'll be happy to come to your office and unburden myself, but I'm not asking you to be a psychologist for the moment," Maggie said. "You know a lot of people from all walks of life, and I'm wondering if someone you know would be willing to break into a residence to clarify a situation."

"Situation? I suppose this has something to do with your Ship of State, or Ship of City, some shoal you need to avoid to keep the vessel off the rocks? This isn't some kind of custody question for your practice?"

"No. Yes, something about the city or maybe about the Ship of Maggie."

Louise paused to consider. "You're serious? You need a break-in artist?"

"Yes."

"Alright. I'll go along with your craziness for a moment. I'm assuming this is very important?"

"Life or death, but not mine, hopefully."

"Alright," Louise said, "I'm reviewing in my mind who among my many acquaintances is stupid and crazy enough to do what you're asking. Let's see. Stupid, crazy, and so, probably, also obnoxious and foolish. The only one I can think of is my son-in-law, Ash, and that even emptier-headed sidekick of his."

"You think a professor of logic and statistics and his friend, a professor of anthropology, would be good burglars?"

"Please don't ever tell anyone, especially not Suzanne, but her husband has been known to resort to this kind of activity. I suppose it's like a rich man or woman shoplifting."

"So Ash," Maggie said. "I'm a little dubious. Don't you hate him a lot?"

"Oh, yes. A remarkably horrible man."

"Would you be willing to talk to him on my behalf?"

"Oh, no. I'm not in the mood for a criminal conspiracy today. You'll have to do that yourself."

"Fine," Maggie said, "We never had this conversation."

Feeling more rational in the morning, Maggie decided she had not yet reached the point where desperate action must follow a desperate situation.

Louise must think I'm insane, Maggie thought. So what? She's known me since childhood and she's probably always wondered about my mental health.

Eating a sweet roll, cherry jelly in the middle, while sitting at her desk in her law office, Maggie felt altogether better, enjoying the sameness of routine. Her father always said that things would look better in the morning, and it was always true.

Thinking of family, she experienced, unbidden, a pleasant memory about her late husband and their courtship. She knew it was an old fashioned word, courtship, but that's what it was. He'd won her over, showed himself to be the man with whom she wanted to spend the rest of her life.

If only . . .

Her cell phone burbled. She automatically answered. On the other end, she heard, "Wally here."

Where is here? Not there? I thought he was supposed to be downstate. "Oh, Mr. Wally, how nice to hear from you. Is this the promised call where you've set up a meeting with one of those three you mentioned? I thought we'd have our little discussion first about whether I'm hiring you or not. I'd be a little surprised if you've already taken the initiative." Of course he had. The man was manic.

"Ben Edelton hired me for you. The Speaker is paying my fee. I thought I told you that."

No you didn't, you impossible man. "How kind. I must remember to give him a buzz and express how I feel." What heinous act will I be forced to do for that favor?

"I've set up an appointment with Michaels. You know, the one with the supremely influential family in your district, who you've never met and probably know nothing about."

Oh, that Michaels. Thinking she might consult an on-line encyclopedia or some other available Internet source about Michaels, she asked, "What is his first name?"

"Don't know. I'll ask around and get you that information before the meeting, if possible. The appointment this afternoon at his estate."

She couldn't help the irritation creeping into her voice. "This afternoon! Don't you think I have other duties, must deal with situations?" She didn't want him to think she wasn't important enough to have a full calendar, even if she probably didn't. "I haven't even reviewed my meetings for the day. I'll have to check with my paralegal. Just a sec." She held the phone away from her and yelled "Harper!" This would give her a few moments to decide what to do.

The young woman appeared.

"What's my schedule for this afternoon? I may have to cancel a meeting if it's not critically important." Here, Maggie had a choice. Gesture to Harper that she didn't want to take the appointment Mr. Wally offered or to indicate that this non-existent meeting was too important to miss.

Harper's eyebrows went up in indecision. What unspoken message was Maggie sending? She couldn't tell because Maggie's face kept changing expression. Maggie herself couldn't decide if she wanted, out of curiosity, to meet with this mysterious, everybody-but-her knows him, Mr. Michaels, or never meet with him.

Harper decided that she was being signaled that she should say that Maggie was available. "No problem," she said, unfortunately loud enough to be picked up by the cell's receiver.

Clicking sounds on her cell indicated another call. "Suzanne Ashley", spoken call waiting announced.

Maggie realized it was too late to torpedo the appointment with Michaels, because Mr. Wally must have heard what Harper said. At least she could take this call and delay, while she gave this matter more thought. "I've a call on the other line. Do you mind hanging on? This might be important." Because you aren't and I am.

"Of course. No problem," Mr. Wally said.

Maggie did the required clicking of her own on her cell. "Suzanne? I'm on the other line so I'll have to get off quickly. What can I do for you today? I talked to your mother just last night. She's fine."

"Yes, I know. She called me right after and begged me to call you to find out what's going on. Mother seemed upset that you were upset about something."

"Oh, it's nothing." But seemed like everything. Maggie had a thought. "Would you do me a big favor? What are you doing this afternoon?"

"Depends on what time. I do have some early afternoon appointments with patients. What time exactly? I don't think I can do lunch. What time are you thinking?"

"It's not lunch. I would like you to come with me to an appointment. It would help me a great deal to have a sane person's perspective. I'm not exactly sure what time. Will you stay on the line and if I disconnect you, could you call back in five minutes?"

"Sure."

How much time did she waste on phone call courtesy? Probably not enough, because she knew how nettled she became when someone pulled this trick on her. "Thanks, I should be able to bounce back and forth until we work this out."

Maggie pushed a button on the cell. "Mr. Wally?"

"No, it's still Suzanne. Try again."

"Sorry." Maggie tried again to shift back to her other call. This time successfully. "Mr. Wally, are you still there?"

"Yes. It's me."

"What time is this appointment?"

"Two p.m., precisely. Mr. Michaels has a very inflexible schedule."

Mr. Michaels is probably a very inflexible man, Maggie thought. "Sorry, I've got to work out the time with the person on the other line." More clicking. If she was this frantic about setting up an appointment, what would the appointment itself be like?

"Suzanne?"

"Yes, it's me."

"Could you come to my office and we'll drive together to a 2 o'clock appointment? I'd really appreciate it and you'd find out what's going on."

"I'll just pencil you in as another patient this afternoon. Where are we going, exactly?"

"I'll call you back as soon as I know."

"Is this a formal occasion? What should I wear?"

"I'm going to dress as if I'm going to meet a rich uncle."

"Fine. Bye."

Relieved to only be talking to one person, she asked Mr. Wally for the details of where she should go to meet Mr. Michaels.

Her destination was an estate on the lake, much further north of Brunswik, but still on the North Shore. "Just identify yourself to the guard and tell him you have an appointment. The guard may be overzealous, I'm afraid. The last time I visited, I was physically searched for weapons. I don't think you'll be searched. Unless there is a matron."

Reassuring. Maggie had a vision of being strip searched by a female jail warden.

Chapter Sixteen

How much of a threat is a 4 foot, 10 inch, skinny old lady?

Maggie decided not to inform Suzanne of the possible search. For one thing, it was absurd. It wouldn't happen. Neither Maggie nor Suzanne presented the aspect of a terrorist.

I can't frighten a cat, Maggie thought. And Suzanne is trained to seem innocuous, until she tells her patients what screwed up little jerks they are.

If she were Suzanne and was told she might be searched, Maggie was certain she would open the car door and jump out onto Sheridan Road, even at 45 miles an hour. Adding her crumpled body to the picturesque old trees on every lot and the lake on the other side.

They reached their destination.

"Good morning, ladies." A uniformed guard stood at a gate that could be swung up and down, like at a railroad crossing. He gave them the once over. He was a burly twenty-five years or so, which made him junior to both in age and senior in bulk. "Please exit your car and walk to the designated area to the right. A matron will search you."

Suzanne looked like she was going to jump as high as she could. Which wouldn't be too high before she hit the ceiling of the car's interior.

Maggie was only consoled by the thought that this could be the most humiliating episode in her life and everything else thereafter would seem less terrifying.

Alternatively, she could just back up and never think about becoming a State Senator. Maybe that was what this was all about? A test to see if she could handle mortification?

"Are you really going to submit to a search?" Suzanne asked. Use of the word "submit", told the whole story. Giving in to the chauvinism and misogyny of some creep?

"Yes." Her curiosity was too strong. "Don't worry, I'll give this guy the benefit of my opinion once we get inside. Hopefully, this won't be any worse than being hassled at the airport."

Suzanne gave a short nod. She must have decided for herself that she would allow a search because she did not want to miss the privilege of witnessing the future wrath of a very angry Littlemayor.

Out of the car and walking to the designated area, they saw a tall, official-looking uniformed woman guard with a gun slung at her hip. Much too young to be called matronly. Her long hair brown was in a bun. She had a pleasant natural expression, which leavened the occasion somewhat. She did not, however, smile.

"Sorry for the inconvenience. If you would walk through the detectors, through the middle, slowly, that would take care of a search for metal weapons. If you have anything of metal on you, not just a wedding ring or a watch, now would be a good time to give it to me." Maggie no longer wore her wedding ring, but did have a ring on the finger that doesn't indicate a woman is married. "No need to take off your shoes. I'll just take your purses."

Maggie handed over her purse with a slow show of reluctance, looking the woman in the eyes until the guard flinched. The woman put both purses on a conveyor belt which went through some kind of boxy mechanism to reappear on the other side.

Maggie led, with what dignity she could muster, through the portal metal detectors. Nothing binged or banged or lit up. Suzanne followed, also without incident.

The woman guard opened the purses on the table and gave each cursory look. She shook up the contents of one, then the other, so she could see what was on the bottom. She obviously didn't want to put her hands into another woman's purse, fearing what? A mouse-trap, a dead squirrel?

She looked at her victims. "If you'll just let me pat you down?"

No, no feeling me up today, Maggie thought. "Absolutely not. We don't have any weapons. We went through your metal detector. If we can't be trusted enough as human beings that we mean no harm, then I don't think we should be going in at all."

The woman guard talked into a speaker pinned to her tunic, and mumbled, probably, what Maggie had said, word for word. Maggie couldn't interpret the garbled sounds that came in reply.

"Please reenter your car and drive into the estate," the woman guard said. "Thank you for your patience." She attempted a conciliatory smile.

Maggie and Suzanne climbed back into the car. Maggie restarted the engine, changed gears to forward, and aimed at the folding gate. The male guard pulled a lever to make the gate rise and smiled evilly at them. Maggie drove the car through the gate.

A long road led to an immense mansion. At the circle driveway, Maggie parked behind an antique Rolls Royce.

They walked towards the door. "My apologies, Suzanne. Thank you so much for coming with me." Thinking to calm Suzanne with some psychological jargon, she added, "This guy we're meeting must be a major paranoid."

Suzanne smiled but said nothing, reserving judgment on a diagnosis, like the professional she was, until all the information was received and analyzed.

Maggie knocked. A dignified older gentleman answered the door. She assumed this was Michaels, but he said, in a *basso profundo* voice, "Mr. Michaels will see you now."

They followed him into a vestibule that led to an elaborate, museum-quality reception room obviously designed to be used only by wax figures from the 19th century. They followed down a corridor and into an office.

Behind a rough-hewn desk, built undoubtedly without nails by some frontier carpenter, sat the oldest man Maggie had ever seen. Older than Maggie probably by forty years, maybe more. She could only guess.

Maggie had read that people who live into their hundreds seem to reach a plateau of old age, just beyond late middle age. Only the healthy and strong make it to that advanced age, and their faces usually are not so weathered and wrinkled that they seem to be from another species.

Not so, Mr. Michaels. He was weathered and wrinkled, Maggie guessed, to the farthest point the human canvas can decay without actual death. His wrinkles had wrinkles. His skin was splotchy, translucent, raw, and dry, highlighted only by liver spots and melanomas.

It spoke. His voice was high pitched but his vocal cords still vibrated. "So kind of you to join me and so fortunate I am alive to greet you," he said.

If you say so, Maggie thought. She nodded towards him in acknowledgment of his continuing existence. "Thank you for seeing me." What else could she say? Thanks for humiliating us at the front gate. Thanks for not dying as we speak and becoming dust.

"You're probably wondering why I wanted you to come here today." When Maggie didn't respond quickly enough, he went on as if they were having a conversation. "I can see you're looking at the painting above my head."

Maggie certainly had not been looking at any painting, her startled attention only drawn to her host's antiquity.

Michaels went on, not needing a response and, possibly, not being able, in any case, to hear one. "It is a frontier scene and portrays my family's first log cabin. I am going to tell you about my family."

No real choice presented. If you must, Maggie thought.

95

"I am descended from a Scotsman who was fleeing the law and a life without prospect. He came to America as an indentured servant, but escaped before his term was completed. On my mother's side, I am descended from Hessians, who fought against the Patriots in the Revolutionary War, until he saw which way the wind was blowing."

At which point, Michaels stopped distinguishing between himself and his ancestors. "I reached this land as a trapper of beaver for fancy hats. I was a personal friend of Daniel Boone. I sailed down the Chicago River with Louis Joliet and Jacques Marquette in 1674 and traded with Jean Baptiste Point du Sable in the 1780's. I perished in the 1812 Fort Dearborn Massacre. I fought in the Black Hawk War. When the Native Americans, as we now call them, the Pottawatomie were pushed off the land, I prospered, extended my farm until it was the size of Scotland and gave my name to paths that became highways.

"I knew Lincoln. He admired me. He laughed at my jokes and repeated them as if he'd thought of them himself. I fought in the Civil War and spent some months starving in the prisoner of war camp in Andersonville until I killed my guard and escaped. I returned home and invested in railroads.

"I survived through every technical advance and economic depression. I saw the rise of strange political philosophies and watched them decay and become replaced by others, even stranger. My political philosophy was my family. I built my home and added to it. I watched what was done to the land and profited from it. I always bought land in the path of progress.

"I was a king. Men rose and fell at my discretion. All that occurred, only did so after I approved."

The old man gasped for breath, and Maggie saw an opportunity to speak.

"That's very impressive, Mr. Michaels. I appreciate that your family has lived here so much longer than mine. On the other hand, as my father would say, my people had a great civilization, arts, science, and philosophy, when yours were painting themselves blue."

Michaels seemed unabashed by Maggie's chutzpah, or in her specific case, hubris. His lips twisted upward in either a smile or grimace, which revealed some very brown teeth, or stubs thereof.

Where did they dig up this guy, literally, and is he about to drag me down to hell with him?

"I understand you are ambitious." He didn't wait for a reply. "That's fine. I will support you for State Senator, but only on the condition that the proposed shopping mall in Brunswik is never built.

"Why?" Maggie asked.

"Because that's what I want."

Chapter Seventeen

"You heard that too? I'm not making this up, imagining it?"

"I heard it," Suzanne said. "Do you talk to a lot of people who are clearly delusional? Is that part of the job of a mayor?"

Now I've discouraged Suzanne, Maggie thought. She'll never run for political office. She gets enough of people with strange ways as a psychologist. Or does one need to be a psychologist to deal with the people who annoy mayors? Would being a psychologist be a plus?

They drove back from the Michaels mansion. Suzanne declined an offer to stop somewhere and get a nice cup of tea. "What I don't understand," she said, "is what this is all about and what does it have to do with a shopping mall?"

Welcome to my world, Maggie thought. "So you don't feel I'm in some kind paranoid loop?"

"No, not paranoid, exactly, more like the victim of someone else's obsessions. What are you going to do about it, or is this the kind of thing you just ignore? I didn't actually hear you say you would go along with opposing the mall. You just kind of nodded and then shook your head in one motion, so that Michaels, if he was able see you, wouldn't know if you agreed to do what he asked or not."

"You've just observed the essential political gesture, the politician who agrees with both sides," Maggie said.

"Whose on what side? I often ask my patients, suggest to them, that they draw a line down the center of a paper and write down who is on either side of a personal issue. As in, my stepmother, sister and brother

98

are against me and, in the other column, my mother, other sister and father are for me."

I could try that, Maggie thought, if my hands weren't steering back down Sheridan Road. "Well, trying that mentally, on the one side are those who want the mall. These would be Matalokus the developer, Rauptt, the head of the Planning Commission, and, of course, the ghost of the late Alderman Casey. On the other side, I now clearly see only that Michaels is against it, for reasons unknown. Does it mean, since Michaels has a relationship with the Speaker of the House, the entire political establishment of the State of Illinois is against the project? I don't know yet."

"Who else?" Suzanne asked.

"Lots of people who live nearby don't want it to happen. Lots of businessmen and store owners do, and the mall would be convenient for some shoppers."

"Where do you place yourself, which column?"

This drew Maggie up short. She had to consider. "If enough of voters in Brunswik become sensitized to the issue and therefore become disaffected with me, then, as Mayor, I would have a problem. On the other hand, Brunswik will survive and prosper either way and the life of ordinary residents won't be affected one whit, mall or not."

"That's how you feel as Mayor. How do you feel personally about it?"

"Angry. What infuriates me is that some people are apparently willing to kill other people for what can only be a profit motive. Money."

"What can you do about it?"

"Not much. I'm not a police person. I've got police trying to catch Casey's killer. Some people obviously think I've got some clout, but I don't necessarily believe that anything I do will make any difference in whether or not the mall is built."

Rightfully suspicious: "You don't have any financial incentive? You won't earn any more, or, sorry to ask--I know the world isn't pure--- there's nothing coming to you under the table if the mall is built or not?."

How wonderfully cynical, Maggie thought. Maybe Suzanne would indeed make a good mayor after my current problems destroy my political career.

"No, not a penny. Besides, do you think I'm Mayor for the money? It pays $500 a year and office expenses. It has no benefits like medical insurance. This is a step up from when the mayoral position was strictly as an unpaid volunteer. I'm only Mayor because of an altruistic flaw in my personality."

Suzanne laughed. "Well, what else is on your mind? Your daughters?"

Pleased to change the subject. "Tracy is possibly about to get engaged. I'll know soon. She's introducing me to her new boyfriend Friday night."

"That's wonderful! I envy your being close to a daughter. Louise and I have, as you know, less than a satisfying relationship."

"Much like the relationship," Maggie said, "as the one I have with Kimberly. That's a whole other story. Remind me to get some advice on that the next time I try a rapprochement."

"No problem. So you haven't met Tracy's boyfriend? Do you know anything about him?"

"She said he was handsome, and I got the impression they've been dating for a while. It's a big step, introducing your husband-to-be to your relatives, isn't it?"

"It can be," Suzanne said. "Sometimes wonderful because you know how much the young man will be liked and eventually loved by your family. Sometimes it's more of a bitter pill because you realize your cherished one violates one of your family's cardinal rules. Wrong religion, color, and/or sexual orientation."

"Thanks, now I'm hysterical. I'm sure she said her potential mate was a guy. Not that I couldn't learn to accept a her if she makes Tracey happy. What was it like when you introduced Ash to Louise?"

Suzanne pitched backward in her seat as if physically struck by her memories. "It was like a declaration of war. You know, there's nothing intrinsically wrong with Ash. He's very smart, very responsible, is loved by his students. Is a good father."

"But?"

"There's an odd strain of irrepressible irony in him. That's the closest I've come to understanding him, and it's my job to understand people."

Maggie thought, Ash is just a little off, something just a little crazy. A little cruel perhaps? She was afraid to ask if he was a mean person.

Suzanne answered her unspoken question. "He's as kind and loving to me and to the girls as anyone could ask. Just that he has this obnoxious side he isn't afraid to show to people. I mean, he's bright, very bright and that makes him somewhat intolerant."

"What does he think of me? Be honest," Maggie said.

"Oh, he likes you a lot. Admires you. I think he'd like to be mayor one day. You know, he's on the park district board. He thinks the other board members are monkeys. It's just that he needs to feel, I think, that he's taking some responsibility for the community."

Oh great, Maggie thought. I'm hoping Suzanne will be the next mayor and Ash is thinking he should run. Being Mayor certainly isn't a job for an obnoxious person, just the opposite. A Mayor must be conciliatory, though appearing strong.

Remembering her intention for bringing up the subject of Ash, Maggie said, "I've asked Louise whether she thinks he might do me a favor."

Suzanne held up her hand. "Stop. Louise hinted that you are thinking about taking some direct action about something. Is it this connected to the mall business?"

"I'm afraid so."

"I won't discourage you or encourage you. But I don't want to hear about it. I don't get involved in Ash's little adventures, especially with that friend of his. Ash thinks, because he occasionally is a consultant, with me, for the Chicago police, that he is some kind of super policeman. I don't want to know about it. I love him and

I don't want him to change. I just hope he keeps out of trouble and so far he has."

They'd reached Maggie's law office, where Suzanne had parked her car.

They both exited. Suzanne kissed Maggie on her check. "I wish you were my mother. I worry about you. Don't do anything really bizarre, unless there is no other way."

"I won't, dear, I promise." Suzanne walked to her car. She turned and waved. Maggie waved back.

I wish, Maggie thought, that she was my third daughter. I love the other two, but Suzanne is like Louise without the barbs.

Maggie walked into her office building. She climbed the stairs to the second floor rather than riding up with a disgruntled constituent. She greeted Harper, who was too busy to talk.

In her office, at her desk, she fished the address book out of her purse, where it was in a unusual place, having been shaken to see if it was hiding a gun or explosives.

She found Ash Ashley's name quickly, being under, of course, the A's. She dialed the number.

"Hello, it's Maggie Wellington."

"Maggie the Mayor?" Ash asked.

"That's me."

"How are you? Suzanne said she would be spending some time with you today. She didn't know what to expect. Did it go well?"

"Splendidly. Exactly as I expected." Insanely. "Are you available for a while? In your office? There's something I want to ask you."

"I'm here, with the door shut and a sign on the door telling students I'm in Florida. Between lectures."

"May I come and visit? Oh, and is your [almost saying, crazy] friend, the professor of anthropology also in."

"Yes and yes. This sounds important. Is it?"

"I honestly don't know."

Chapter Eighteen

"Missing," Detective Smith said, breathing into the phone. "That's what I said, Rauptt is missing."

"I thought you said hissing," Maggie said. "Oh, I shouldn't joke about this. You say no one has heard from him?"

"It was reported to the police that no one answers his phone. He missed all kinds of appointments last night without calling to excuse himself. His car is in its parking space at his condo building. The janitor wants to know if we want to get inside. Said he would allow us in without a warrant if the police thought there was some kind of medical emergency."

Maggie was in her law office. Harper had been waiting, standing at her desk, poised to talk when Maggie's phone rang. She'd gone back to her desk and started another project.

"Chief Feather feels it is too early to break in," Smith said. "Wants to wait the usual amount of time. You know, to make sure the missing person hasn't just gone off somewhere in a romantic haze."

Rauptt really isn't the type, Maggie thought, to go off for a wicked weekend. "I wouldn't be concerned, except that Rauptt," she tried unsuccessfully to suppress the urge to say a final "tuh" at the end of his name, "is so careful about his appointments, so, if you don't mind me saying, so anal about everything. I think there must be something seriously wrong. Maybe he really is ill?"

"I can't overrule the Chief. Only you can. I'm just giving you a heads-up. If you want someone to look into his condo, you'll have to inquire on your own to Feather, and please don't mention me."

"I'll do that."

Maggie broke the connection and pushed the speed-dial number for Chief Feather.

When he realized with whom he was talking, Feather said, "Good morning, Madame Mayor."

She knew this mock courtesy of calling her "Madame" was some kind of put-down of her or some kind of boost up of his ego. He was again, to his regret, dealing with a hysterical woman, one whose emotions ruled her. Someone incapable of the kind of rational thought that his own, superior brain generated.

'I've lost someone."

"Who?"

Playing dumb, she thought. "Our soon to be alderman, Rauptt. He was supposed to be at a meeting last night and didn't show up or call in. That's so unlike him. I always worry when a person who lives alone gets sick and may not have a support group to watch over him."

Does Feather even know what a support group is? Men tend to downplay the connections they have in life, she knew, preferring to show how ruggedly independent they are. Feather had a support group in his wife and children, although he would have argued that he was giving them the support, rather than getting support from them.

"We ordinarily don't just rush out every time someone forgets to call in with an excuse." Feather said. "You can see how that would cause chaos on the force." You ninny, Maggie mentally interjected, finishing his sentence in her own mind. "That's all we'd be doing. Checking on the secretaries who oversleep. I understand, these days, that the schools will call to check if a child is absent for more than a day. That's got more to do with child abuse."

Why was this really bothering her, that Rauptt wasn't answering his phone, why? Obvious. Yesterday she given less than an enthusiastic response to a demand to jettison the mall project, and today, one of its staunchest supporters is among the missing. Just like you-know-who.

Maggie said, "I rather think that being so active in city government puts Mr. Rauptt in a similar category.

104

Government official abuse. Rauptt has been involved in a project of some controversy. If any harm has come to him, we need to know as soon as possible."

"A public official is still a resident who deserves his privacy. Although, this reminds me of the time..."

"I'm sure this is a very illustrative example from your undeniable experience and expertise, but I think being a public official is a bit of a waiver of privacy. Holding yourself out as a public figure, changes the rules. Listen, if I wasn't answering my phone, even if I was merely in a funk, someone would be knocking on my door within an hour, demanding my attention."

"If you want to give me a direct order to investigate, go to Rauptt's condo, I certainly will do that."

"So ordered. I'll meet you there."

"I'm a little busy right now, with duties that can't be delegated. I'll send a Lieutenant, if you don't mind. He can make any decision that's necessary, with the necessary authority."

Feather must have meant a small "l" lieutenant, Maggie thought, when she met Detective Smith in the front vestibule of Rauptt's condo building. A person "in lieu of" rather than a police official.

"Feather sent me, because I'd been involved first," Smith explained.

Maggie was glad that it was Smith and not some stuffy administrator. "What should we do first?" she asked. "I don't usually spend my mornings breaking into residences."

"The first thing we need to do is take a look at Rauptt's car. It's in the basement parking area, and we can get there by taking the elevator down. If we see any signs of violence, no matter how small, we'll have a perfect excuse for entering his premises."

The elevator doors were already open. The elevator was so small, it barely held the two of them. Smith pushed the "G" button, the doors closed and the elevator lurched into life, apparently pulled by some unseen hand from below.

Maggie read the framed license in the elevator which noted an inspection about three months before. Maggie knew who the inspector was by her initials. A conscientious person. So even if this elevator was operated by a mule at a wheel below, the elevator would probably function correctly as they descended and would lift them up, as well, when the car inspection was over.

Smith read off his notebook that Rauptt's car was in Slot 25. He led to a dark Mercedes-Benz. The very small, expensive kind. Maggie said, "I never realized that Rauptt is such a sport." Why do men choose cars to compensate for personality deficits?

Maggie followed Smith's example and circled the car. Smith had a flashlight and focused the beam on the inside of the car, especially on the driver's seat. The car was meticulously clean. Smith said "I wonder if this car has been purposely washed, inside and out, to hide evidence?"

Maggie had no opinion. It was possible that Rauptt always kept his car without spot. That must be why, when they had that luncheon appointment, Rauptt had driven separately to the restaurant, when he could have, just as easily, picked up Maggie at the entrance of city hall. Maybe Rauptt didn't want female Mayor cooties on his upholstery?

"I'm going to break into the car," Smith said. He withdrew a shiv from an inside pocket. He put it through the rubber mounting around the driver's side window. He jiggled it about until he hooked the mechanism, then pulled.

Maggie was about to ask Smith why he wanted to get inside because they had made such a thorough inspection from the outside. Smith paid no attention to the interior. He quickly found a button that released the trunk.

She belatedly understood. Smith wanted to see if Rauptt was in the trunk, dead like Matalokus' brother. A chill ran up her spine as Smith raced around the car and opened the trunk fully.

His flashlight scanned the inside of the trunk.

106

Smith shook his head. "No Rauptt, thankfully." He slammed down the trunk lid. The sound echoed throughout the lower level.

"Now what?" she asked.

"Now we take that little elevator up to Rauptt's condo and I use the key the janitor gave me. Then, if he's not there, we'll close the door and no one will be the wiser. It will be our little secret that we checked on Rauptt. He's probably at a convention for some thrilling hobby, like collecting stamps or exotic seashells."

Back in the elevator, Maggie asked "Which floor?" Smith pushed the "3" button. They rode up quietly, as if their presence would be discovered and an alarm would spread throughout the building.

The door of Rauptt's condo opened easily. Which meant that he probably was not in. If he'd been present inside, he would have drawn the chain across or turned the second lock to prevent even the janitor from molesting his sanctuary.

They saw, down the corridor, that a light was on. Which didn't prove anything. Most people, Maggie thought, liked to leave a light on to discourage burglars.

They moved down the hallway to the bedroom.

No one was there and the bed was made.

The condo didn't even feel very inhabited. It was super-clean. Rauptt was not just anal, he was super anal.

"Well, what do you want to do? He's obviously not here," Smith said.

"I'm not quite done snooping, if you don't mind. It's always interesting to see how someone you know lives. Let's go into the family room or maybe that would be called the living alone room in this case. I want to see if there are any family pictures.

They padded back on the thick carpet. On the mantel, Maggie saw a picture of Rauptt and the woman identified on the sign-in sheet as Mrs. Matalokus.

Chapter Nineteen

"I'm hearing rumors," Becky said.

Calling as Maggie drove back to her office from Rauptt's condo. Maggie felt frustrated because she wanted to give Becky a look of surprise and annoyance, but couldn't do so through the speakerphone system of her car. She'd need to rely on the irritated sound of her voice.

Coldly. "For instance?" Maggie asked.

"Something about the head of the Planning Commission. He supposedly went off to some hubcap collecting convention but was waylaid by a gang of kidnappers, who have sent in a ransom note to the city, asking for five million dollars."

Wow, Maggie thought, news not only travels fast, it travels imaginatively wrong. Smith must have had just enough time to joke with another officer about Rauptt's whereabouts. That info traveled like wildfire to some other officers, each adding his own bit of fanciful conjecture. And on and on with the speed of light, until it reached Becky, the nexus of all gossip.

"All I know for sure," Maggie said, "is that he missed some meetings last night and isn't answering his phone." True as far as it went. "Don't you think it's a little premature to be suspecting a full scale drama, complete with a ransom note? And why would the note be sent to City Hall? He's not a ward of the City of Brunswik, just a volunteer. Rauptt must have a family and they must have money if he's worth kidnapping, don't you think?"

Why didn't the ransom note get sent to the mystery woman in the picture? Because the kidnappers didn't know who she was, either?

"I see what you mean. You're right. It's all probably just a premature rumor. I'll hold off on writing anything. The deadline for the paper isn't until midnight tonight for the Saturday edition. If someone does give you a ransom note, could I ask you to tell me?"

"If that happens, and I can't imagine why it would, I'm sure the police wouldn't want to make it public. It might get Rauptt killed, if for some unknown and unlikely reason, he has actually been kidnapped."

Chagrined, Becky said, "You're right. What was I thinking? I'm sorry, I haven't covered too many kidnappings, or actually any, so far."

What suggested kidnapping, exactly? "Do you have any idea, on the basis of the rumors, why anyone would kidnap Rauptt?" Maggie asked.

"Me? No. The word going around is that he knows something about the Alderman Casey murder slash arson. Rauptt worked a lot with Casey because Casey oversaw the Planning Commission."

Maggie found this to be an interesting connection of dots on a map of complete ignorance.

Becky went on. "But to change the subject to why I really called, I think I may have found someone, a very nice gentleman, although I haven't met him, who could be your date for the triple with us, Harper, and our intern."

Here it comes, Maggie thought. The fix-up of the century with some doddering old codger. Hopefully not Michaels. "I'm very reluctant to discuss this. These fix-up things are usually disastrous. An evening with some old guy who has saved up everything on his mind since his wife died and wants to take this opportunity to unload to a woman."

Becky laughed. "I can imagine, but, no, this is someone the intern guy knows, a family friend. A man recently retired, edging 70. Greek."

The best thing to do at this point, Maggie thought, is to throw my cell phone out of the car window, before it gets me into more trouble.

Becky wasn't done. "A very nice man, does a lot of volunteer mentoring with young people. Was a successful lawyer, sat on Boards of Directors."

109

Maggie drew air into her lungs, but couldn't find the words. Such as no or yes.

You only have to be lucky once. That's what her mother had said about finding a good man. Maggie had been lucky once and maybe that was her limit, all she could hope for in this life. Being lucky twice seemed like an excess of good luck. On the other hand, it would be nice to have a man around the condo. Someone who could do home repairs, drive in wintry weather when she was frightened by the threat of black ice. A man who could appreciate a good Greek meal.

"I'm not agreeing to anything. Why do you think this wonderful older gentleman would want to go out? Is he a widower, or what?"

"A long time widower. Newly retired, probably wants to find a mate before it's too late. Is receptive to only being fixed up. Won't use the personal ads."

"Too late" was the only phrase Maggie heard. Too late for this kind of foolishness. She was too set in her ways. Not interested in a new romance. "I'm not saying no, but I'm far from saying yes. When would this triple be?"

"Saturday night."

"Impossible. It's already Friday. Shouldn't he at least give me a call to make sure I don't think he's a mass murderer?"

"I admit there isn't a lot of time. But he could call and you could decide."

"I'm not saying yes and I'm not saying no." What was it about dating that made a person feel so insecure, adrift and dumb?

Becky's call was interrupted by a call from Detective Smith. Here was an opportunity to tell him to keep quiet. He should know better. She apologized to Becky and switched over to talk to Smith. "Marcus, have you been talking to people about Rauptt? I've got a reporter on the other line who seems to have some actual knowledge among the exaggerations and lies."

"Not from me. You know, though, once I report in, I can't vouch for the security of any information.

110

People do overhear things. I wish I could tell you that police men and women don't gossip. We're all so pushed together at the station, it's hard not to know everyone's business."

Ah, so I'm at fault, Maggie thought. I should be providing better accommodations for Brunswik's finest. "Well, the harm's been done. I think I've held off the reporter for a few hours. Why are you calling?"

"I've found someone who knows about the murder of the Matalokus brother, and he might, given the right incentives, tell us what he knows."

Incentives? Pay for information? Not very appealing. "How reliable is this guy? Is he someone off the street?"

"No, he worked for old man Matalokus in St. Louis when he had the restaurant. Claims to know what got the brother killed."

Maggie considered. As soon as this man was brought in to see her, the rumor mill would begin to churn. She no longer thought she could conduct the Matalokus investigation with anonymity. Too many people were becoming interested.

Besides, paying for information seemed conspiratorial and demeaning, like she'd descended into a world of lies and innuendo. If Smith had ways of getting people to talk, that was his business. "I tell you what. You find out what he knows, check out the reliability or feasibility of what he says and do it off site, not at the police station. When you are convinced that the information is legit and relevant, come with him to see me at my law office."

"Will do," Smith said. He broke the connection without saying good-by. Becky was back on the line. Maggie prayed Becky hadn't heard what she'd said to Smith. Hopefully, Maggie hadn't established a conference call when she thought she was switching to the other line.

"I'm back, Becky."

"I'm still here. Was that about the ransom note?"

"No, nothing so immediate or newsworthy. Cat in the tree, barking dogs. Maybe we can talk later?"

"Alright, but what do I say to Mr. Senior Citizen Dreamboat?"

That he should sail off to a different sunset, Maggie thought. "I suppose he could call me, but tell him what a bitch I am so he isn't surprised when I hang up on him."

Will she argue the point that I'm a bitch? No. "I will," was all she said, before breaking the connection.

Her cell phone burbled yet again. Maggie was nearly at her office and considered whether she should just ignore the call. She decided she'd better pick up. Maybe the call was from the kidnappers.

Almost as bad as hearing from the kidnappers, it was Mr. Wally.

"You made quite an impression of Mr. Michaels," he said immediately, without any of the niceties and preliminaries of talking to a friend.

"Really? He made quite an impression on me as well. Is he all there, mentally?"

Irritated by the question. "Yes. I hope you'll take whatever advice he gave you. I hope you aren't getting cold feet about running and will follow his every suggestion."

Or what? All my aldermen will be killed or kidnapped? "I took his comments very seriously."

I hope that is a satisfactory answer, she thought. Ah, how sweet to be a politician and never actually answer a question.

"Excellent!" Mr. Wally apparently wanted to put a good spin on her answer and reacted to the imaginary answer he wanted to hear rather than the one he got.

"Anything else I can do for you, Mr. Wally? We're having a bit of a crisis here in Brunswik. You understand, the Mayor is always dealing with crises. Cats in trees, barking dogs."

"Of course, of course. I need you to visit Senator Markham. It's got to be tomorrow, Saturday. I hope that isn't an inconvenience, but he's at the Brunswik Hospital awaiting his removal to hospice care."

He wants to talk to me before he dies or so that he can die? Or does he want me to euthanize him?

Chapter Twenty

Other than her daughter, Tracy, who should she call to get an idea what to wear to a life-altering event?

"Louise, I'm in a panic. What should I wear to meet my daughter's probable fiancé-to-be?"

"You should dress informally but elegantly. I'm thinking business casual with just a touch of old-fashioned mother. Your make-up should not overwhelm but accent your better features, such as your experience-filled eyes. I suppose you've gone to the hairdresser this afternoon and don't look like a hekdish, which I'm reliably told is Yiddish for 'a mess.' You are going for a wise, yet loving look. Kind of like the Good Witch of the North Shore, a woman of nobility and no-nonsense, tempered with love."

"I stopped listening after your use of the word that means a mess. You think I'll be a mess, and this young man will reject my daughter on the theory she'll look like me in 35 years? I'm especially nervous because this didn't happen at all before Kimberly got married."

Louise knew what Maggie meant. Maggie hadn't the opportunity to meet Kimberly's intended, Brad, before he and her daughter married, because they eloped. Maggie was still sad she wasn't allowed to attend her daughter's wedding. Brad was Episcopalian, a nice man, steady, an electrician, and a very good father, so she could not really complain. She was still learning to love him.

"Let's be serious," Louise said. "If he loves your daughter, he should be more worried you won't like him, that he'll be one who is inappropriately dressed. He's got to impress you, not the other way around. No one expects a mother-in-law to be anything but a discombobulated relic from another century, so if you are less than awful, by one bit, he'll consider himself lucky."

Maggie did not feel reassured. "Is that how Ash felt when he met you?"

"Ash is an exception to every rule. When we met I was perfectly dressed and he was disheveled. Years of living with Suzanne have improved his hippie ways and now he's just repugnantly dressed. Here's a comforting thought. This youngster has got to be a better specimen than Ash."

"I'm still not feeling more confident."

"Listen to your oldest friend. You are a wonderful woman, someone any man would be proud to call his mother-in-law. You've created this wonderful woman who this young man is crazy about, and he should be eternally grateful. Straighten your lines and fly right. You can do this. Be calm. Center yourself. Deep breath. Let it out slowly. Think of how happy you were when you first held Tracy after you gave birth."

"I'll try. Thanks for the pep-talk."

"Call me the moment you get back to your condo and give me the details. Every last one."

"I will and thanks. I do feel better." Good old Louise. She'd heard, for decades, every last one of Maggie's private thoughts on the world and other people. She was the one continuous person in her life.

They said their good-byes as if Maggie were leaving for a particularly horrific task and might not return in one piece.

Maggie looked once more in her closet and slid several dresses aside, so she could see others. This one, she thought, makes me look wise but not too old, still attractive, well-preserved but not like a prune.

As for accoutrements, she wore her trademark scarf and also chose silver earrings and a necklace her late husband had given her on an anniversary of importance. In a way, she thought, I'm taking him with me to meet the future of our family.

That brought tears to her eyes.

Maggie did not remember driving to the restaurant but came back to reality as she handed her car keys to a valet. "Thank you, ma'am," the probable college student said. "Aren't you the Mayor of Brunswik?" Not waiting for a reply. "My mom worked in your campaigns, Elyse Halperin."

"Elyse." Who the heck was Elyse? "Of course. How nice. Tell her I said hello." He was already in the car and shifting it into gear. He gave her a "see you later" wave as he drove off.

The maitre'd also knew who she was and gave her a slight bow and a smile.

Who was she? The Mayor of Brunswik. Her private life as a widow and mother was her secret identity. Would the two personas clash?

Would the young man be astounded if an irritated constituent interrupted to complain? To balance that, maybe a few of her law practice clients would stop to say hello and praise her enthusiastically? Helping, rather than hurting, her reputation? Perhaps an old friend would come up to say how much one of her kindnesses had meant to her and her family?

Too bad she couldn't orchestrate the entire evening.

"Oh, yes, the Wellington party," the maitre'd said. "Some have already been seated. Come this way, please."

Maggie walked past others who were waiting for tables. One woman gave her an envious look. She'd probably been waiting for an hour. Maggie hoped this woman wouldn't be giving her dagger-like looks all evening.

Too bad for that lady, but rank does have its privileges. Tracy, recognized as one of those Wellingtons, must have been shown to her table with her mystery man as soon as she walked through the door.

Tracy sat at a square table in the middle of the room. A handsome young man stood when he saw Maggie coming.

How nice. Courtesy. At least Louise had been right to that extent: he wasn't Ash.

116

Tracy took a step between the standing man and her mother and gave her a warm kiss on the cheek and a fast hug. She extended one hand towards the young man and the other towards Maggie. "Mother this is James Wagstadtler."

He gave her a careful, not bone crushing, handshake, as if Maggie were a fragile old piece of crystal. "I'm so glad to finally meet you," he said.

Her smile widened in reply. At least he was taught some manners by his mother, Maggie thought.

He was a very tall man, perhaps a head and a half taller than she, and Maggie hoped she didn't appear to be child-like in comparison. Tracy was at least six inches taller than her mother, having received ameliorative tallness genes from her father.

James moved to draw out Maggie's chair, waited and pushed in the chair for her to sit. What to say to start? "I love this restaurant."

Mistake! She didn't want to turn the conversation to being about her. Don't focus on herself. She was here about her daughter and her fella.

"You look wonderful, mom." Maybe Tracy sensed her mother's nervousness?

"Thank you, sweetie. Let me look at you." Tracy wore a bright colored outfit as only a young woman could. Her hair was perfect, but her joy at being there with her intended and her mother was what made her beautiful. "You look wonderful, dear." She couldn't stop herself from whispering, "Am I appropriately dressed?"

Whispering back, "Oh, yes."

Tracy commenced small talk. She used the word "we" in describing the joint activities of herself and the young man. Speaking for two, the new social unit. The as-yet-unsanctioned by the Lord or the State religious and legal unit. Already a duo. Tracy and James. James and Tracy. Mr. and Mrs. James Wagstadtler. Mrs. Tracy Wagstadtler.

James had a kind of expression on his face that was both expectant and reluctant. He was waiting for Maggie to speak.

"It's so nice to have you home for a while," Maggie said, talking directly to Tracy because she still felt too shy to address James.

"It's strange but nice to be back after so long and to talk to old friends. Our hotel is wonderful," Tracy said. "We have a few more days, then it's back to work. James is starting a new position in the company. He'll have a corner office and several assistants."

James smiled and preened. He doesn't want to appear to be bragging, Maggie thought, but he can't help it. Just a man with a little boy inside.

"That's wonderful!" Maggie said. Finally speaking directly to him, she asked, "Will that mean a lot of traveling for you, James?"

"No, less. We will probably find a house in Hartford after . . ." He stopped because he didn't know how much Maggie knew about their wedding plans.

It's gone that far, Maggie thought. What happened to asking the parent for a daughter's hand in marriage?

Her late husband, Martin hadn't asked either. Maggie still wasn't sure that he had even proposed to her or if she'd just dreamed up that event later in talking to her friends. They were just, all of a sudden, planning a wedding. He just told her he loved her and that was that.

How did James compare to her beloved husband? Not so well. He didn't have the same twinkle she always saw when she looked at Martin. He didn't seem to have Martin's inner fire.

That was unfair, she decided. She'd only seen Martin through the illusionary glass of love. She didn't know James at all. He must have very good taste if he loved her daughter.

"James is Greek on one side," Tracy said to answer an unasked question. "His mom is Greek and he went to Greek school after day school, like Kimberly and I did."

So James identified as Greek. Maggie knew that she shouldn't distinguish between her daughter marrying someone who was of Greek heritage and anyone else of any other ethnic extraction, but, there it was. Everyone feels most comfortable with the way they were raised and the traditions that warmed them.

"We hope to marry in a Greek Orthodox church," Tracy said.

Maggie's imagination filled. Tracy, resplendent in her wedding dress, and James standing nervously before the congregation, then breaking into a smile when he saw her.

Maggie felt suddenly very close to her late husband and felt that he was smiling too. She relaxed considerably. She knew what to expect now.

She wanted very much to meet James' mother as soon as possible. So they could embrace and wait for grandchildren together. Sit together at Church and at funerals.

"Is your father still with us?" Maggie asked. A kind of ungraceful question, but what would be the right way? Is your father dead?

Sad, appropriate look, "I'm afraid not." He took a breath. He was a good son. "Dad passed away last year. Mother is very pleased about our getting married." He hesitated. Had he make a mistake by telling her they'd informed his mother before the mother-in-law?

Maggie wasn't insulted. At last, some good news. She couldn't wait to tell Louise. As the mother, Maggie had a lot to do before the wedding. Certainly, she would have to host a pre-wedding dinner. She'd select an appropriate dress for that occasion and for the glorious wedding itself. Oh, how she'd dance!

"Where, what city, will the wedding be?"

Tracy said, "Here. Brunswik. Most of my childhood friends are still here, and the rest of my friends and James' friends will just have to make this a destination wedding. Chicago is a fine place to get married."

"Yes, it is. When? Have you set a date?"

"We figured," Tracy said, "that we better coordinate that with you."

I may die right here on the spot from happiness, Maggie thought.

Tracy's cell phone rang. "Hello." She listened.

"It's Kim," she explained. "Ethan broke his arm and could I go to the emergency room to be with them?"

Chapter Twenty-One

Exhausted. Returning home from the emergency room at midnight. Really no strength to call Louise. Too late anyway. Better to call her tomorrow. Needed to.

She wanted to tell Louise that the engagement part of the evening went well, but the emergency room episode left her wishing she had a better relationship with Kim.

Maggie remained irritated that her younger daughter had asked for her sister, not herself, in a time of need. She'd gone to the hospital anyway. Worse, Kim shook off any attempt by Maggie to engage in a conversation.

She'd learned the story about the accident from Kim's husband, Brad. Ethan had fallen from a slide in the backyard and fractured a bone in his lower arm, when he tried to break the fall. It was a simple break, according to the doctor's interpretation of the x-ray. Ethan would need to wear a cast, but not for that long, although Maggie knew several weeks was like a lifetime to someone his age. She'd need to visit with a special present and kiss him many times.

Home at last, she'd listened to her voice mail. No word about Rauptt's fate. Nothing further about Alderman Casey, except an official report on the arson. Feather would send a copy to her city eMail.

Also, a message from Becky. She wasn't writing anything yet about Rauptt. This was the decision of her editor. She complained that, by the time the bi-weekly was printed again, Rauptt would likely be old news or already found unharmed. In other news, the fix-up date fellow would call Maggie tomorrow.

Sleep came fitfully. She worried about seeing the dying State Senator Markham in the morning. While in the emergency room at Brunswik Hospital, she'd thought of also visiting the ailing Markham, who was in a room three stories above. Killing two birds with one stone, so to speak.

Not really a good idea, she finally concluded. Visiting hours were over anyway, and she didn't quite know what she would say to him if she had to wake him up: "I decided to come twelve hours early, in case you wanted to die tomorrow in peace or were waiting to die until after you saw me."

To think of more pleasant thoughts, had she liked James? He seemed very strong and consoling at the emergency room. He sat next to her several times and made polite conversation. He said his mother would call her soon to make whatever wedding plans were necessary. She was looking forward to meeting Maggie, he said.

James had an older brother and a younger sister. He was the middle child. She'd only had two children herself, so Maggie tried to remember what the magazine articles said about middle children. Let's see, the oldest child is a leader, the youngest is spoiled. The middle child is neglected but independent.

Her phone rang at 7 a.m. Louise. "I couldn't sleep anymore without getting the postmortem." Maggie forgave her friend for waking her from a coma-like sleep, because she badly needed to sort out her impressions from the previous night.

"What's Mr. Right like?" Louise asked.

"Tall. Polite. Half Greek but identifies as Greek."

"Oh Maggie, I'm so happy for you." Louise wasn't Greek, but knew of the strong family ties in Greek families.

"His mother is going to call me today, he said. She's the Greek half. His father has passed away, so it will just be the mothers who have responsibility for the wedding. I'll give you the date as soon as I know. I'm sure it won't be for several months, but I bet it's a beautiful fall wedding."

"I can't wait. How special."

"Thank you. I think so too. Oh, but there was one shock during the evening."

"Tell me."

"One of my grandchildren, Ethan, who I call the 'great, good soul', fell from a slide and broke his arm. Kim called when we were at the restaurant, so we all went to the emergency room. Which was fine. Ethan will be fine and will heal right up. Being in the emergency room gave me an opportunity to get to know James. He is a nice boy, a middle child between an older brother and younger sister. Middle children are independent, right?"

"All generalities are suspect, but let's decide this one's true. Independent and self-sufficient is good. But sometimes the middle child needs a lot of attention and love. Does he seem like a kind person?"

"Yes. Very kind." Long pause. "Sorry, I'm falling back to sleep. I'll call with more details later in the day."

Nothing until breakfast, which was a stale roll with butter, because she hadn't shopped for a week and had used everything else up in her refrigerator. She assessed the mess in her condo and decided she could wait until Sunday to clean.

She retrieved her city e-mail and read the arson report. Nothing much new. A staged grease fire, with the grease so far from the fryer it must have been scooped up in a pot and thrown to the corners of the kitchen by deliberate hands.

How does one dress up for a meeting with a dying State Senator? With dignity and respect. She spent what seemed like an hour deciding which outfit would show concern and interest. Something, she thought, that doesn't say I am an opportunist hoping you will die soon so I can start being a State Senator.

She parked on the third level of the hospital's attached parking lot, which was open to the sky. Fortunately, the day was bright and clear with no rain in sight. She felt the sun on the back of her neck as she walked towards the elevator and wondered if she had finally lost her winter paleness.

The volunteer lady at the desk gave Maggie a map to Markham's room, marking the route in yellow. Pointing, "You'll be taking this elevator when you get to this spot. Sorry, but the hospital has had so many additions, it's impossible for you to just guess where to go. Be careful. Look at the signs. Occasionally there's a sharp incline when two additions don't quite meet up."

Maggie thanked her. She was glad the volunteer hadn't recognized her. She didn't feel like being social or political until her mind cleared a bit more. She walked past the hospital coffee shop. She decided to buy some tea and carry it with her. Unfortunately, the tea was too hot, even through a cardboard sling around the cup, and she dumped it in a receptacle, without taking a sip.

Walking, she trudged up where two wings met, badly. She took the correct elevator, unless she was reading the map upside-down.

After the final turn, she saw a nurses' station. A nurse nodded at her, too busy to care who was visiting.

A man in an express delivery uniform brushed past her, his arms filled with flowers. He turned his head to read the sign on the wall that the 3300 wing was in the direction of the arrow. She followed him, since they both seemed to be moving in the same direction.

The delivery man arrived at Markham's room and walked in. Maggie waited outside, to allow the ailing older man to accept the flowers.

At least one person cares whether he lives or dies, Maggie thought.

No one else seemed to be in the room and no one stood waiting outside the room. Such as a nervous and worried family member, being stoic as their beloved relative's death approached. The lack of entourage for the dying State Senator seemed incongruous for a man who had probably spent his time in office surrounded by staff and hangers-on.

When the delivery man exited, he looked distracted. He held a small computer and pushed on the screen, apparently to register the delivery. On a tight

124

schedule, Maggie thought. Was it really that important that things arrive quickly? Whole industries thought so.

Still outside the room, she said, "Senator Markham?" To give the man some time to cover up if he wasn't. "Hello, may I come in?"

"Yes." He had a weak, high pitched voice. Maggie remembered that he was in his late 70's, not so really old these days, but obviously someone who would not ever regain his health.

She entered the room. The flowers had been placed hastily aside on the movable tray table.

Beyond the flowers, Maggie saw Brunswik through one wall of glass. The city was brilliantly bright and looked very rural and green from this high above, with many trees and gardens.

The neglected flowers bothered her. Honestly, was no one helping him?

Best to tell him who I am, she thought. She couldn't be sure he would recognize her. For one thing, he wasn't wearing his glasses. "I'm Maggie Wellington. We have an appointment." Before he could reply, she said, "Let me get those flowers into a vase for you."

She found an empty vase on a ledge, grabbed the flowers, and walked into the small attached bathroom to draw some water. Ugh. She personally would have dreaded using such a cold and antiseptic washroom.

Maggie stripped off the foil that surrounded the bottom of the bouquet and placed the flowers carefully in the vase. Would the vase tip from being top-heavy? No, the vase was bottom-heavy enough to act as a counter-weight.

She placed the vase on the window sill, where it looked splendid. There, he can look at the flowers and be cheered, she thought.

Maggie sat in an uncomfortable guest chair and drew it close to the bed, careful not to disturb the tube that dripped liquid into his arm from plastic bags and the wires apparently attached under his gown to his chest.

125

"We've met several times before, Senator. I'm pretty sure we were both at the dedication of one of the new wings of this hospital. Do you recall?"

"No." He obviously was having some trouble getting his words out and could only answer monosyllabicly.

"Mr Wally," to drop a name, "said you wanted to see me. I confess that I'm interested in being a State Senator some day, which I hope is far in the future and your current health set-back is overcome." In other words, I'm waiting for you to die. Maybe I should just say that and be honest. No, this was one instance where honesty was the worst policy.

Great effort on Mr. Markham's part to speak a sentence. "I need to tell you something."

"Yes." She leaned forward, encouragingly. Maggie realized for the first time in her life that encouragement meant to give courage.

"I'm willing (gasp) to endorse you as my appointed replacement, (gasp) but first, you must listen to Mr. Michaels and veto the mall project."

Should she explain that the project was approved long ago by the city council, that she had not even cast a tie-breaking vote because the vote was unanimous, and that the mall project was in abeyance, in any case?

Wanting to avoid a tiring discussion or a debilitating argument, she said, "I'm certainly learning to take Mr. Michael's advice." There, a good variation on her dissembling prior statements. "Could I ask why the project should be canceled?" Why, why, why?

"Because," he gathered up his dignity to make a profound statement, "No one willingly gives up power." He closed his eyes and was thereafter unresponsive, but breathing.

Chapter Twenty-Two

Maggie answered her personal cell phone. She'd taken a long nap after talking, if that was a conversation, with Senator Markham. She sat in her kitchen in the condo and was glad no one could see her, because she probably looked half-asleep and needed to reapply her make-up.

After a long moment, a deep masculine voice asked, "Is this Maggie Wellington?"

"Yes." He must be the mystery man who would chat her up, as the British say, and ask her out. We teenagers sure have fun, she thought.

"Um, I'm Harold Mola. I was given your number by your reporter friend, who thought we might go out on a triple. It's tonight, which I know is short notice, but there really isn't time for a coffee date, which I hear is the way that young people do it now."

Maggie inwardly shuddered, afraid she would sound a little hysterical with so much going on in her life. She could do this, she told herself. "I knew you were going to call. Why don't we just ask each other questions like we would if we were having a coffee date? In fact, I'll go and get some tea, if you don't mind?"

"Great. I'm so bad at this. I haven't asked a woman out in 40 years. The whole dating thing is so different than when I met . . ." He'd obviously been told not to mention his late wife until much later in the relationship, so he wouldn't scare off the victim of his romantic interest. At least he's trying to be honest, if not totally succeeding, Maggie thought. "I'm pretty rusty. I tell you what, if you don't mind staying on the line, I'll go pour myself a cup of coffee too and I'll talk from my kitchen."

Why is important that he talk from the kitchen? Maybe he feels most close to his late wife where she used to putter. Maggie could only imagine how messy a widower's kitchen would be, lacking the diligence of a wife. Maybe he wanted to remind himself that he needed someone to take over and clean up the kitchen and was too cheap to hire a cleaning service. Wives clean for free.

"I'll be back on the line in a moment," she said. "If we get cut off, call again."

"Hello, I'm back," he said

"Me too. What would you like to know about me?" Maggie asked.

"Your reporter friend has filled me pretty much. You must work very hard and have very long days as a mayor."

He does have some empathy, she thought, but does he just want to know if I'm too busy to even talk to him? "Being mayor is really a very part-time job," she lied, not wanting to scare him off either.

She took a breath. "My crises are usually in the category of cats caught in trees or barking dogs. The rest of the time, I specialize in custody matters and advocating for the educationally handicapped." She thought to ask him what his specialty was when he worked, but nixed that, not wanting to imply he was past his prime. "I understand your practice includes being a Board of Director for corporations?"

"Yes, I did extensive corporate law before deciding there was more to do in life, but I'm still active on some Boards, because they refuse to let me retire, and I also do some pro bono for non-profits."

"It sounds like you're still a busy man." Turn around being fair play, maybe he's the one who is too active to be dating?

"Yes but I've still got a lot of excess time and energy." Which might mean, what? He needs a playmate, someone who would let him escort her to plays and operas or travel with him to exotic places, at his convenience and without any emotional attachment?

Or maybe he spends a lot of time with his family? I don't even know if he has a family, she thought. I certainly don't want to put up with the rigidly set ways of an old bachelor. "Do you attend a lot of family functions, you know parties?" Lame, she thought.

"Yes, I have one son who has two sons, who are both musical and athletic. I'm always going to musical recitals and tennis games. I won't let them play brain-bashing games like football or other contact sports."

"That's wise. I would worry a great deal about head injuries." See, I read the newspapers, and I'm a warm and compassionate person as well.

"Our reporter friend says that you are an extremely young grandmother."

I wouldn't, she thought, call myself extremely young, but I suppose it's a matter of perspective. "I have two daughters. One is married and has two children who I am trying to spoil." Uh-oh, did I give away that there is some animosity between my daughter and myself by using the word "trying"? He'll think I'm an old bitch. Change the subject. "My older girl has just announced her engagement. I am so excited."

"That's so wonderful! I wish I were closer to my daughter-in-law, but she just doesn't seem to like me all that much. I do everything I can."

Those words out of his mouth, he's probably already recriminating himself for bringing up something that isn't cheerful and ideal. He must really have this problem on his mind a lot and would sincerely be grateful if someone with a woman's touch could help him with his problem. That's kind of an interesting challenge, since I can't do much with my own daughter, Maggie thought. At least he's not saying he is perfect and is trying to be somewhat open and vulnerable.

"I find that a little love and diplomacy goes a long way," she said. I hope he doesn't think I just insulted him, that he's an idiot with people. "Of course, It takes two to tango. If the other person is just unresponsive to all overtures, it's best to just keep away from her." Good recovery.

"People are always a challenge, but that's one of the things that makes life interesting." Her translation: My wife used to take care of interpersonal relationships, all birthdays and social occasions.

He continued. "You must meet all kinds of people in your work?" Fishing for other relationships? Like other suitors. Yes, I'm bombarded with requests from potential suitors. But she said, "Yes, they are a great source of insight and friendship." Did I just make him feel bad that he doesn't have more friends?

"I've met all kinds too, and I play golf with a group of old guys."

He's saying he is not a hermit and is considered normal by his contemporaries. She wanted to ask, how old is old to him, but didn't want to intimate that she herself was too old. "That's wonderful exercise." Are you a healthy old geezer?

"My golf game has actually improved since I retired." He's saying, he's as healthy as a thoroughbred horse.

Ask him about being Greek. Try to find commonalities. "Were you born in the Chicago area? Maybe we've crossed paths or know each other's friends."

"I was born in New York, and we moved to Chicago when I was a teen. We went to:" a list of Greek Orthodox churches.

"Really, what a coincidence. I went to several of those churches growing up. Maybe we have met in some distant past."

He laughed. "Maybe we did."

I think I've broken through his shyness, Maggie thought. It's his turn to ask me who I know. She enjoyed doing Greek geography. For instance, "Did you know" so and so, "and the priest" at such and such?

He asked her about her life in Chicago's Greek community, and they both remarked about a mutual acquaintance.

Maggie said, "Small Greek world, isn't it?"

"It sounds like we have a lot in common. Would you like to be part of this triple date? The logistics sound a little overwhelming."

He really needs someone to help him socially. Is that good or bad?

"It sounds like fun." Why not go out with him? "I will work out the details with the other women."

I really want to find out, she thought, if this guy has bad personal hygiene or lets his cat climb in trees and kicks his dog so he barks at midnight.

Smith marched in a very old man into Maggie's mayoral office. Thick white hair instead of being bald, but with a wrinkled face. "Maggie, this is Mr. Stephanopoulos."

This man gave her a small courtly bow and said with a thick Greek accent, "Hello." He was very old world, a link to the past, someone who only fit into a world long gone.

Maggie felt nostalgia for the generations that preceded her. So warm, so full of life. Such humor. Gone now.

"Mr. Stephanopoulos believes he knows why the Matalokus brother was killed," Smith said. "Isn't that right Mr. Stephanopoulos?" The old man shook his head, yes. "He worked for many years at the Matalokus' restaurant in St. Louis. He was the night manager."

Mr. Stephenopolis nodded again and smiled proudly. It was a mark of honor to be left to run the restaurant, the precious family business, to be so trusted. Much less common than the usual. Most sentences about the fill-in manager start, "The son of a bitch robbed me blind."

Smith continued. "Why don't you tell us, in your own words, what you think caused the brother to die."

"I can tell you. The brothers, between them, was bad blood. The old man, maybe he played favorites, nothing I ever saw, but the two spoiled boys hated each other. They were very upset about who inherited what. That's what I think. One boy killed the other for the money."

I hope Detective Smith hasn't paid this man too much, Maggie thought. This story is the second oldest in the Good Book.

Chapter Twenty-Three

From a Chicago newspaper website, at 3:12 p.m. after she informed Chief Feather at 2:14 p.m. that a ransom note had been pushed under the door of her condo:

A Brunswik official was kidnapped Thursday night, the Morningstar has learned exclusively, and is being held for ransom.

Despite efforts to suppress reports, sources close to the Brunswik police confirmed that Edgar Rauptt, the chair of North Shore community's plan commission, was kidnapped when he returned to his Brunswik condo.

Sources stated that Rauptt's car was found in the condominium building's underground garage, with no signs of a struggle. Police speculate that Rauptt was abducted on his way up to his condo unit, either at gun point in the elevator or in the corridor outside his third floor unit.

Details of a ransom note and the amount demanded for Rauptt's safe return are being withheld, pending investigation. The ransom note was pushed under the door of an unidentified city official's residence in Brunswik and was found after she returned from a Saturday morning appointment.

Police searched Rauptt's condo after the ransom note was received.

Police provided no opinion about why the ransom note was sent to the city, rather than to Rauptt's family. Rauptt is a city volunteer, although a prominent one, and police did not immediately know whether the kidnapping was related to his official duties.

As chair of the planning commission, Rauptt was the liaison to the Brunswik City Council on matters of new construction and applications for building permits. His appointment to fill a vacancy on the Brunswik City Council has been rumored.

Most recently, Rauptt supported a shopping mall project in Brunswik, but police expressed doubt that his involvement had anything to do with his abduction.

Little is known about Rauptt personally, although it is speculated that he is the creator of a popular computer program, who became wealthy after the sale of the program to a conglomerate.

His early history before becoming a prominent Brunswik volunteer is unknown and a search of Internet sources shows no listings, police sources said, except for his Brunswik activities. On this basis, it is speculated that Rauptt may have changed his name to maintain his privacy or previously used a business name to maintain his anonymity.

Evidence in Rauptt's condo has alerted Brunswik police to the possibility that Rauptt has or had a wife or sister, according to sources who asked not to be named, and efforts to contact this person have been, as yet, unsuccessful.

Police urged anyone with knowledge of the kidnapping to contact their local police department. Brunswik police are coordinating the investigation with other North Shore suburban departments. Calls to the police non-emergency line in Brunswik or any of the neighboring suburbs will be quickly followed up, according to Brunswik Police Chief Anthony Feather.

Brunswik Mayor Maggie Wellington was unavailable for comment. A city spokesman promised a statement from the suburb as soon as more information becomes available.

The ransom note, although technically asking for no money, was simple. *"Do what you know you need to do or you will never see Rauptt alive again."*

She wondered what exactly she knew that she needed to do?

Obviously, this was some kind of reference to the shopping mall project. The damn shopping mall project.

Like what could she do? It was too late for her to kidnap or kill Matalokus. He was already missing. Too late for her to kill the project's chief sponsor on the city council. Some arsonist and murderer had already done that. It was too late for her to kidnap Rauptt, the only one who could have put the deal together to continue the project.

She could go to the city council and say, "Unless you all want to die, we have to reconsider having a new shopping mall." That seemed like a strange thing to say, bizarre words to come out of her mouth. Maybe, she could make this suggestion in closed session, but a council reconsideration vote on the issue must be taken in public.

How would that play in the local media? "Mayor Loses Her Sanity."

She could just be honest: "If this project is completed, my personal ambitions will be thwarted, and I will never have even the merest chance of doing good in the world. Or being able to look back at my life with any satisfaction. So, therefore, I must ask you, the city fathers, and you, the citizens of Brunswik, to make this sacrifice for me."

She doubted that the average alderman or the average person on the Brunswik streets cared what happened to her political career.

How about lies? "It has come to my attention that, geologically speaking, a giant sinkhole is forming under the property designated for the shopping mall project."

Alternative lie: "If we dig there, a giant entrance to the netherworld will open and we will all be dragged to hell. Or worse."

Thinking about "average" and "Brunswik" in the same sentence reminded her of a question she'd often asked herself. How big, population-wise, was ancient

134

Athens when it produced such profound art, philosophy, ethics, architecture, even democracy itself?

Probably the size of Brunswik, which has produced hobby art, pseudo-philosophy, situational ethics, ugly architecture and the city government of Brunswik, which may or may not be a democracy, but probably is not.

"Really mother, I'm handling it," Kim, the self-sufficient, stubborn and hostile daughter said.

"I'll just drop in, if you don't mind?" She had about an hour before she had to prepare for the triple date. "I won't stay long. I just want to reassure myself that Ethan is on the mend. I have a little present for him, and I'm sure it will cheer him up."

"If you must. What's your estimated time of arrival? I've got a lot to do and I've got to start getting dinner together."

Why can't your husband help you once in a while? Maggie knew not to ask that question. Pointing out any imperfection of or lack of support from Kim's husband, always made her daughter's temper flare.

"I'm at the toy section of your local pharmacy. I can be there in no time."

"Alright. I'll listen for the doorbell."

Driving up, Maggie saw Kim's house. Maggie always thought it looked a little old fashioned, cookie-cutter similar to the other houses on the block, and totally uninviting. This neighborhood had never been the wealthiest part of Brunswik and was only slowly becoming more upscale. Maggie had provided the down payment, but had never been specifically thanked for her generosity.

Maggie followed the cement walkway to the front door. She rang once. No response. She was afraid to push the button twice, not wanting to be accused of being pushy and aggressive. Her daughter would get to the door when she damned well pleased.

The door opened. Kim gave her an automatic smile, then realized she was being too pleasant to her awful mother. So she frowned. "Come in. Come in. Ethan is in his room." I wash my hands of you. Do what you want. "I've got something on the stove." Kim rushed away, leaving Maggie to find her own way to Ethan's room.

Both Ethan and Evan were named after Maggie's mother Evelyn, passed on these many years, their great grandmother.

Evelyn had been a very modern mother for the times. She'd clung to traditions but encouraged Maggie to find her own place in the world. She'd always been supportive of everything Maggie tried to do. During the brief time Evelyn was still living during Maggie's marriage, her mother showed great love and respect for her son-in-law and was very helpful with advice about their little daughters.

If only, Maggie thought, she could have the same relationship with Kim.

Maggie found Ethan sitting cross-legged on the floor. How he was able to kneel in that position, then sit, with only one arm to support himself, she could not guess. It must be because young people were so incredibly agile.

"Hi, Yah-Yah." Maggie loved being called the Greek endearment, although sometimes she felt like looking around to see if her grandchildren were actually addressing the phantom spirit of her own mother. She bent to give him a kiss on an upturned cheek.

This was all that was real in the world. The love of a child. Loving a child. The rest was meaningless.

Chapter Twenty-Four

Wanting to present the best possible Maggie, she spent quite a while looking at herself in the mirror. Which depressed her.

In that instant before her face changed into its public mode, she saw a haunted old woman. Rejecting that image, she smiled at herself and decided she didn't look so awful, still had a lot of charm and verve. Looked like she still had some juice left in her, some fire.

All this build-up for what would be the let-down when she actually saw the antique who would be her date? Still, one never knew, the world being full of hope as well as sorrow, if one would meet a soul mate.

Another soul mate? Why not? Maggie did not believe that only one person in all the world was meant to be hers. That fate created one perfect mate for her, and she'd already had hers and lost him. She thought, that given the chance, she might have made the precious concessions that had to be made so she and someone else, not the man she'd married and mourned, could bear to live with her as husband and wife.

That give and take, the adjustments and small deals between partners, still attracted her interest and left her breathless. After all, concessions work both ways, and it was an intoxicating thought that someone might actually go out of his way to please her.

Becky called. "How are you dressing?"

How does one dress for a night at the movies and a dinner at a restaurant that was one step above fast food? Certainly not formally. A fun outfit. Summerie and casual. For a fun evening, without any pressures. Hanging out with the posse. Except that most of the posse was so young they could have been her children.

137

She gave Becky the benefit of her opinion, leaving out the irony.

Logistics had been agreed upon. Harold would pick her up at the condo, and they would meet the others at the movie theater. She told Becky, "I haven't been keeping up on the popular movies this early before the Oscars. Is this one in contention and will there be a crowd?"

"No, it's more of an art house movie with," whispering into the cell, "very little sex, in consideration of you and Harold."

Whoa! Did Becky assume that people of her advanced age of 66 no longer were allowed to even look at sexy images? What exactly did young people think old people were like? That they would avert their eyes and think of something more pleasant, like cashing a social security check? "I'll try not to run out of theater screaming if there's some kissing."

No perception of irony or sarcasm. "Good idea. Oops, got to go, Berry is growling."

Maggie finished putting on her make-up. Not bad, she thought. Not so bad at all. What did this Mr. Mola look like? Hopefully, he wasn't one of these men who refused to look their age and had gotten hair implants and jowl tugs, and end up looking unnatural. Personally, she would never go that route. Her mother had grown more beautiful as she got older, and her grandmother's face had been a book upon which all was written.

The doorbell buzzed. The worse thing about a first date is not knowing the routine. Was Harold supposed to come up after being buzzed through the security door, or was she to descend grandly into the vestibule?

"Hi, it's Harold. Should I come up or do you want to come down?"

Coming up meant that he might see the inside of her condo, which she still hadn't cleaned. If there was a second date and she'd had time to tidy up, she'd invite him up. "I'm ready and I'll be down in just a few more

138

minutes." Let him figure out that she wasn't so ready. It's a women prerogative to take her time to prepare.

"I'll be waiting."

She grabbed a shawl in case the air conditioning in the theater was overwhelming. She wouldn't put on the shawl until he received the full impact of her outfit. She gave herself a last check in the mirror.

Riding down in the elevator, she tried to refocus her mind away from all that had occurred in her life recently. It was a night for socializing and discovery.

Mr. Mola wasn't exactly a disappointment. He didn't look like one of those movie stars who just got more distinguished as the years went on. He just looked liked a normal person. He had a nice smile. Perhaps, he wasn't exactly a dreamboat. Probably not "a cute guy" in a teenager's imagination but acceptable nevertheless.

Harold was tall and would need to stoop a little to kiss the top of her head, if he should ever be so inclined. He still had a thick head of hair, grayish, mixed with plenty of what must have been black hair. Also, Harold had thick eyebrows. Maggie liked thick eyebrows.

"Hello." He held out his big paw to gather in her diminutive one. He had strong hands but was very gentle with hers. He was treating her a little like she would break, but she knew she could breach his reticence, if she wanted. "So nice to meet you finally, face to face," he said. "I suppose I've seen your picture in the newspapers, but, I live at little further up the North Shore and I don't get to see all that much of Brunswik politics."

"So nice to meet you, too." What was missing? Even her father knew to compliment her mother when they went out for the evening. No compliment had been offered as yet and it left her in doubt. Had she made some style or fashion error? Did he think she looked hideous or what?

A smile lurked around his lips as if he knew this was all a great, amusing game. Like he would tell her a joke, and she would laugh. Maggie liked a sense of humor above all.

He speaks! "You look lovely."

139

You, sir, have made the correct response. No matter how old she would become, those few words of appreciation would always be so important. It wasn't just that she looked good, it was that a person wanted her to feel good, was happy to be in her presence.

"You look pretty good yourself, big man."

He laughed.

This is going to work out fine. At the least, this will be a pleasant evening with a man I've never met who could become a friend. At the most, it might be the start of something good. Ah, optimism.

He knew he was being inspected. "I'm not quite over the hill," he said, smiling, "and you are definitely still climbing up to a peak."

How incredibly sweet to say that. She mentally reviewed the faces of every man she'd talked to in the last week. Sweetness was not among their attributes.

"Shall we go to my car?" The carriage awaits.

Harold opened the outside door for her, courteously.

Damn, she thought, I think this guy wants to sweet talk me until he gets into my pants! An odd thought, dragged up from her subconscious, but a pleasant one. Something left over from her teenage dating days.

He opened the door of his car to let her in and waited until she sat and began to draw over the seatbelt. He shut the car door soundly but not with daunting force and went around the car to sit in the driver's seat.

"Um, am I dressed alright?" He was in a tailored shirt with a checkered pattern and a tab collar. Open at the neck, his shirt revealed some manly body hair on his chest. He wore expensive blue jeans.

"You are perfectly dressed."

Harold was slim, did not have a paunch. His waistline wasn't midway up his chest like some older men. He still looked a little athletic and probably had some muscle inside his shirt. His arms, exposed by the short sleeves of his shirt and raised to the car's steering wheel, looked powerful, and his hands adroit. "You'll have to be patient with me. I'm afraid all my dating savvy is from a different geologic age. Like when there were dinosaurs and it was fashionable to carry around a club."

"I hope you'll just relax. I know this is your first date in a long time, but I'll try to get you through this, if you'll let me." Not such an unpleasant feeling to be needed.

He nodded, and said, simply, "Thank you."

She looked at him from the side. He did have some personal dignity. He did look intelligent and worldly-wise in many ways, although, probably from what he'd said, he wasn't very wise socially. Which was fine. She could work with that.

"Next stop, the theater and our young friends."

Chapter Twenty-Five

Exercising their prerogative to go to the ladies room as a herd, Maggie was questioned by her young female friends. Not exactly at the height of elegance, the washroom of the very informal restaurant was at least clean. No other patrons were present.

Harper asked Maggie, "What do you think of Harold? He seems like a fine man. Like my father." She hesitated. "I'm giving him a compliment here."

"I haven't made up my mind. He isn't awful," Maggie said. Who knows what Harold is really like? He's trying his best to present his idea of what kind of man I would like, not being himself at all, she thought. Only occasionally did he provide a brief insight into the real man.

"I like him," Becky said, checking herself in the mirror, "but, of course, he's not my date. At least, Berry is being his sweeter self. He likes Harold and they've been discussing the Cubs. That's the male equivalent of advanced socializing 101."

Maggie laughed. "I think Harold is doing well for someone so long out of the dating game."

"How about you?" Harper asked. "You're not quite your effervescent self, either."

"Really? I better start effervescing." Maybe a giggle would help the next time Harold attempted to be witty?

It's just that Harold was trying too hard. Or was she over-interpreting?

Despite his nervousness and over-attentiveness, Harold had been somewhat quiet and reflective during the movie. Was that the real Harold or was that just simple politeness?

He'd gasped along with the rest of the audience during the part of the movie where the heroine is in danger. When the heroine sacrificed herself for the good of others, he may have shed a tear, but she couldn't tell because he looked away, perhaps purposely. She'd been tearful, herself, so she really couldn't get a good look at him.

Despite all the attention he gave her, Maggie doubted that Harold liked her all that much. He would have been the same with any generic woman.

Would she accept a second date with him? Probably, just to see if he loosened up in her presence, with familiarity. A third date seemed highly unlikely. The second date would probably be enough to help him through the trauma of dating again. Then he could find some woman more to his liking.

Leaving the ladies room, also in a group, they resat at the round table between their respective men.

Maggie took a good look at Eric, Harper's date. He seemed like a very bookish man. He'd probably not become a litigator. He didn't have that, standing on the balls of his feet, kind of energy.

On the other hand, Eric obviously was very intelligent and most likely very kind. He was not an extrovert and Maggie wondered if he wasn't so far up on the introvert scale that he wasn't, just a little bit, suffering from Asperger's Syndrome. Well, there was nothing wrong with introversion, after all. The world must be made safe for the introverted. They contribute so much creativity.

Berry seemed a little uncomfortable with where the conversation was heading. As if the detective feared he would reveal a police secret, he purposely changed the topic away from the crime in the plot of the movie to the latest escapades of Cubs. He brought up recent changes in the line-up and whether the recently named coach would last out the season. Maggie did not know the previous line-up and didn't know the current coach's name.

Harold seemed to like this discussion but Eric kept quiet, true to his introversion. In his favor, he tried to look interested in sports talk, but Maggie thought Eric's mind was elsewhere, choosing, perhaps, a topic for an article in his school's law review.

Becky refused, after a few minutes, to be dissuaded from discussing the movie. The heroine was played by one of Hollywood's finest. Unlike most starlets who sparkle for a few years, she had remained popular, based mostly on her extreme versatility and ability to lose her own identity while making the character she portrayed completely believable.

"Wasn't she amazing?" Becky said. "Do you remember the scene at the trial where she stood up to the other lawyer and with one word and one look beat him, almost literary, into the ground?"

Here was a matter upon which Harper could comment. "You know, that kind of grandstanding is just fiction. Most trials I've seen are deadly dull. Just trying to get some favorable testimony into the record, pulling the answers out of the witnesses, who are all idiots. The lawyer plays mostly to a jury made up of retirees and cab drivers, and the judge is usually asleep." When no one immediately commented, she said, "Don't you think so, Maggie?" She obviously wanted to bring Maggie into the conversation so she could have a few moments in the spotlight.

"Yes, very dull," Maggie said. "But, once or twice in a lifetime, a lawyer gets to play the part to the hilt, save the day like the lawyer in a movie. Most of my victories, I have to admit, were of the small kind. A child who gets away from an abusive parent. A student who gets the help he so desperately needs. Much less dramatic, but just as important for the individual whose life is being affected."

I hope I don't sound preachy, she thought. This kind of talk must be depressing for others. Was Harold deciding that she was an alien from outer space and as feminine as a prune?

144

"Talking about lawyers, you might be interested in what happened today," Harper said. Even Eric appeared somewhat intrigued by this change of topic. "Out of the blue, out of nowhere, I got a call today from the managing partner of one of the largest law firms downtown. I would have told you immediately, Maggie, but we really didn't have time because we were both getting ready. This guy said that he had heard of me, and invited me to come for an interview. I'm not even third year yet. I can't image how he heard about me, of all people. As if all the lawyers in town are sitting around waiting for Ms. Harper to graduate and take the bar. Hard to believe."

"I think that's wonderful that some firm is interested," Maggie said. "That kind of break could really change your life. You should carefully consider any offer. I'm not sure what you're learning with me has any real money-making future. After you pass the bar exam, you could move to an outlying area and set up a similar practice. I could throw some clients at you. But my kind of practice will never generate the big bucks."

Harper was clearly moved at Maggie's offer of help in the future. Quite a day she was having. "Well, that's very nice too, your offer to help me after I pass the bar, and I thank you. I will certainly keep that in mind. I can't imagine myself as a high powered Chicago litigator, but it's such a compliment to even be considered."

Looking troubled, Harper added. "Do you think that the strange, really strange, totally strange Mr. Wally had something to do with it? He's the only person I've talked to recently who might have some downtown connections."

Maybe, possibly, could be, Maggie thought.

Was this offer to Harper some kind of inducement that Mr. Wally could dangle to make Maggie more amenable to killing the mall project? Something like, do what you are told and your protégé will go far?

No matter how she tried to distract herself, the mall project kept being injected into almost every part of her life.

Maybe this job offer to Harper was more like a threat? If Harper started her apprenticeship downtown in preparation for becoming an associate after graduation and the bar, it would be a blow to Maggie. Not a devastating one, but still a negative. Maggie could hire and train any number of talented women to help her in her practice. She did, however, have some motherly affection for Harper and would miss her. That couldn't be denied.

Or was she being paranoid? Everything that happens in the world wasn't about her.

The restaurant emptied until only the six of them remained. Fearing the restaurant was about to close, Berry asked the waitress for the check.

Harold, still trying too hard, offered to treat them all. Eric, who was obviously a nearly destitute student, didn't object. Berry, however, wouldn't hear of it, and the bill was split three ways, with Harold accepting cash from the two other men and charging the whole amount on his credit card.

As they made their exit, a woman walked through the door, not looking at them, just reading the menu that was posted over the counter.

Maggie immediately recognized this woman. She'd been with Severn Matalokus the night last June when he presented the mall project to the city council. The possible Mrs. Matalokus. Also, the woman in Rauptt's photo.

How could she get this woman's attention to cross examine her? Maggie was too embarrassed to show such aggressiveness on a first date. Grabbing a stranger was too out of character for her. But maybe she could quickly think up some excuse?

Being in the presence of friends and potential friends discouraged her just enough so she held back. Besides, maybe she was wrong and this wasn't the same woman. Am I, under the strain, beginning to see what and who I wanted to see?

An opportunity lost, but, consoling thought, if the woman was in the area, perhaps Maggie would see her again.

If the woman saw Maggie, she didn't say anything. She continued towards the counter to order.

Next to their three cars in the small lot facing the restaurant was one other parked car. Maggie tried to memorize the license, but lost the last three numbers when Harold said something to her. And later she wasn't sure about the first few numbers and letters either.

Chapter Twenty-Six

"I don't know how I feel about Harold," Maggie told Louise, who was in California for a convention of fundraisers for scientific research. Louise was scheduled to address the group to encourage--there was that word again--them to shake down more contributors. All for a good cause, of course.

Damn fundraising. In an ideal world, all scientific research would be funded by enlightened governments with tax money given joyously by a thankful public.

Of course, the world has its priorities. Very few magazines highlighted scientific research as compared to the many magazines that speculated who was dating who. People seldom gossiped about a scientific breakthrough. Why was that?

"Do you think you'd go out with him on a second date?" Louise asked. "Did he try to kiss you good night, at least?"

"No, but he did walk me to the door. Is current etiquette that I should have invited him in? I was so tired, and he looked pretty beat himself. Besides, I wanted to write down something I was trying to remember, but that didn't work out well either. We just shook hands, but he seemed reluctant to let my hand go, if that means anything."

"Hey, we're talking about mature love here. Handholding may be his limit. His libido may be out to lunch. At our age, we have to settle for companionship, not lust or passion."

"You are depressing me," Maggie said. "I'm personally not too old for passion and even lust. I'm lonely in my bed, already. Of course, if that's all the gentleman can do, a good hug at the right time and some playful time together might suffice, I suppose. But I would be disappointed."

"You go girl! Don't settle for less than what you need even at this superannuated time in your life."

Maggie's mind drifted away from the interrogation about her date the night before. She'd called Smith, woken him up even earlier on a Sunday morning, to tell him to check for car licenses with the number 6 and the letter E. Which was all she could remember from the plates of the car she thought might be the one driven by whoever that woman was.

In explaining why she wanted to know if this car was owned by Matalokus or his wife or even by someone related to Rauptt, she'd been forced to explain all her suspicions to Smith. She'd held back about the discovery of the picture of Rauptt and the mystery woman, because she feared Smith would think she was insane, or, at the least, had an overactive imagination.

Smith had been kind about her explanations, as if talking to a person with extreme learning disabilities. His tone of voice suggested that he thought Maggie was tying things together without string.

Smith's return call broke into her connection with Louise. Maggie apologized and ended her conversation with her friend as quickly as possible. She switched over to Smith on what was probably the third ring.

"Any luck?"

"Maybe, but probably not," he said. "I got some people out of bed who work in the Secretary of State's office, because it's Sunday. Collected on favors. Matalokus owns/owned about five cars. None of them have the portion of license plate numbers you gave me. There's one with a 6 and one with E, but none with a 6 and an E."

If only she'd been able to remember more about the license plate. She'd just been too distracted. Too many people with her, too much to take in mentally, too many impressions.

Holding Harold's hand as they parted had not been unpleasant. He did look into her eyes. Did that mean something? He did have nice eyes, but kind of opaque, so dark that she couldn't see into the depths. If there were depths.

Smith: "I left word with a Secretary of State police hotline to search if there were any cars registered under the name of name of Olivia Matalokus. Or any variation thereof on her first name, followed, for instance, by a maiden name, whatever it is, then her married last name. Olivia, with no middle initial, was the name on the debit card, if you recall. Also, tomorrow, with luck, I'll receive a copy of her driver's license, with her picture on it, of course."

"Good idea." Why didn't I think of getting her picture that way?

Too much going on. Her focus being elsewhere.

Also, she thought, too bad I hadn't remembered the woman's possible first name at the restaurant, asked if she was Olivia. Maggie berated herself. She could have simply asked the woman if she was Mrs. Matalokus.

Maggie's mind had gone blank on names. She wondered if senility was settling in.

Smith continued. "Did you recall what the make was on the car you saw?"

"No, still not. I'm really not up on the latest models. It didn't seem like a luxury car or that it too terribly big for a person her size."

"Sounds like a dead end, then. I'll follow up on the picture on her driver's license, when it arrives. I'll go over to the clerk's office tomorrow and see the recording from the meeting you mentioned. The one where you think this woman appeared. I'll compare what I see to Olivia's drivers license picture--which could be as old as eight years if she reapplied on the Internet--to the woman in the picture we took from Rauptt's apartment. We've got it in evidence. Of course, as I recall, the picture must have been taken many years ago."

"I guess that's all we can do," Maggie said. "Be sure to fax over a copy of her driver's license." Maybe that would be helpful. "Any leads on the arson or the kidnapping?"

"No. There were plenty of spots in Rauptt's condo building that aren't covered by surveillance cameras. This was a residential building, not a bank vault."

Maggie broke the connection with Smith. Official business being completed, she wondered if Harper had liked her blind date with the young man, Eric.

She decided that Harper must be awake and preparing for church, as the both of them should be doing. Maggie needed to give one of the elegies for Alderman Casey. What she would say when it was her turn would probably depend on what was said by the prior speakers. She couldn't just repeat what the others said. She'd need to extemporize.

Maggie punched in Harper's number.

A half-asleep Harper answered, "Is this Reverend McMabe, calling to find out why I'm not in church?"

"Yes, it's me, the Reverend. I suppose I woke you up. Do you want to turn over and call me later?" Maggie asked.

"No, no, I should be up. I wasn't exactly asleep, just day dreaming. What's up?"

"I was wondering if you liked Eric?"

"I liked him fine. He seemed to be a good person. Not exactly the exciting type."

"Sometimes that's good," Maggie said.

"Sometimes. To change to a much more interesting subject, what did you think of Harold?"

"I don't know how I feel about Harold." This was becoming the rote answer. Please, someone, help me to decide if I like or dislike Harold! "Wasn't he kind of bland and conventional? Not exactly a figure of romance. He must be about 70 years old. Not to be ageist since I'll be reaching that milestone in a few years, myself. Harold is a nice guy, I suppose. He just doesn't light a fire in my heart."

"I think you really need to give him a chance," Harper said. "I always tell myself that I can't possibly know anything about somebody I've just met. Sometimes it's the opposite eventually. If your heart went pitter-pat about him already, that could be a false impression."

Harper could be right. Maggie decided to think later about false impressions.

Wasn't she being selfish by not getting more details about Harper and her date? What kind of a friend was she being to Harper? She ought to give Harper the benefit of her own observations. "To get back to your date, Eric seemed like a fine young man to me. A little reticent. An introvert, perhaps?"

"Yes, well, he's very smart. I don't think he'll be an aggressive lawyer. I think that he's forcing himself to engage in life, not allowing himself to hide in a corner. In a way, that's admirable, don't you think? It's harder for someone to be outgoing when it's so against his nature, and he's doing remarkably well." Thinking. "I'm haven't ruled him out. I'm social enough for two. We don't need to both feel like we must make a favorable impression on everyone in the world. He's kind of comforting, in a grounded kind of way."

Maggie knew just what she meant. Her late husband had not been very social or overly friendly. He'd depended almost completely on her for their social life. Occasionally, but rarely, he would befriend someone at work and have Maggie invite the man and his wife for an evening together. It was rarer still for Maggie to like the wife of the co-worker, but it did happen once or twice.

"Wait, now I remember what I wanted to tell you about Harold," Harper said.

"What and when did you talk to have a chance to talk to him?"

"We were walking out. You seemed very self-absorbed, like you were lost in thought. I asked Harold, just to be friendly and find out if we had any mutual acquaintances, if she knew Severn Matalokus."

"And?"

"He does. Or did. He hasn't talked to him for a long time. They did some business together. He didn't say what. I asked him to call and find out what is going on with Matalokus. He said he would. I don't really think he will. He seemed very reluctant and a little embarrassed. Men don't really call business associates to shoot the breeze like women do."

Chapter Twenty-Seven

"No."

"I'm sorry. I must have misheard you," Mr. Wally said through the tiny speaker in her cell phone. She sat at her desk in City Hall. "Did you say you wouldn't meet with our banker about your campaign for state senator, or that you didn't have time to talk to him this afternoon?"

"No. What I meant was that I have no intention of meeting with your banker, or anyone else, Mr. Wally, whom you may suggest." Maggie hoped she was achieving the kind of cold tone she wished to convey.

"I don't understand."

Maggie held the cell away from her ear and looked at it as if she could look into the eyes of Mr. Wally. She heard a scraping sound as she unconsciously pushed her desk chair back. As if preparing herself to jump up and flee. As if putting a physical distance between herself and the cell phone would solve her problem.

"I'm thinking seriously of not running," she said. "The city government of Brunswik seems to be under attack lately. And I still don't know what anyone expects me to do about the mall project. Look, if the intention was to bring the mall project to a halt, it couldn't be more halted, already. Matalokus is gone and Rauptt, the only person who could have put the deal back together, is still missing. You can tell whoever wants to know that it's over. Whatever was so damn important about the mall project is now null and void. Do you get it?"

"I don't know what you are talking about."

Maggie thought about smashing the cell phone onto her desk. At least with landline phones, one can hang up dramatically to emphasize a rant.

Mr. Wally continued. "I really don't think you should give up on becoming state senator. Mr. Michaels was quite impressed with you. As was State Senator Markham. Who has died, by the way."

"I'm sorry to hear that he has passed away," she said. Genuinely sorry, as she would be for the passing of anyone who wasn't, for instance, a mass murderer.

This changed things. His death meant she needed to make a final decision quickly about running. She was still 95 per cent in favor of quitting before she began. The problem was, she didn't think of herself as a quitter.

"I'll call when the funeral and wake is scheduled," Mr. Wally said. "It would be best if you attended and made some kind of eulogy. I'll have someone write one for you. Also, I'll have his chief senatorial aide call you, Parsons. Perhaps you could hire him before he's hired by some other candidate."

Way off track here. "Look, I'm telling you I've greatly soured on this state senator business. The people you've sent me to were, objectively speaking, nutty, although I hate to speak ill of the dead or mostly dead."

"I'm sure a lot of your impressions are merely from your lack of experience. Everyone loves you as a candidate. In fact, I believe the party leaders are already coming together to give you their endorsements."

I don't want their nutty endorsements, she thought.

Maybe it was Mr. Wally who was the problem, and there was a glimmer of hope she wasn't losing her mind? "Look, is there someone else I can deal with besides you? Could you recommend some other political operative? Sometimes people are so different they can't work together. It's nothing personal." Yes, it is, she thought. "Do you know what I mean?"

"Yes, I know what you mean. Sorry, you're stuck with me. I was hired by the Speaker of the House and Mr. Edelton. Only they can fire me. If there is something in my manner that bothers you, you should write down what it is and I'll put it in your file. I promise I'll do my best to conform to your image of what I should be like.

After all, I can only advise. The candidate makes the decisions."

Write this down and stick it in your file: Stop being an ass, which you obviously cannot stop being because it is the essence of your being. "Can I get back to you? I'm very busy this morning."

"Of course. The Banker will be coming to see you at your city hall office at 1:15. I strongly urge you to be there and to take his advice."

Maggie broke the connection, feeling just as good as someone who has dropped a downed power line which was causing her upper torso muscles to contract.

Time to go shopping! The Banker could come to her office and read the magazines in the waiting room, but she would be across the city boundary at the giant mall, looking for clothes she could wear on informal dates, such as coffee dates, in case those should occur. She needed some scarfs as well.

If the new mall had been built in Brunswik, she wouldn't have wasted the five extra minutes in traffic to get to the stores. Were those five extra minutes worth dying for? Apparently.

She thought: Should I just call Harold to find out what he knows about Matalokus?

Would it violate some immutable dating rule to talk to him so soon after their date? Would that be way too eager, enough to scare anyone away?

Even if he had been mesmerized by her charms, she wouldn't have expected to hear from him until at least Wednesday. Or had things changed so much? Was the rule now that either of the tentative couple was free to call when the whim whammed them?

It was not exactly taboo to call him, not even illegal. If he didn't want to be called, then he shouldn't have programmed his number in her cell phone. Was that current practice? Probably. She'd reciprocated by pushing her office numbers on his cell after he'd set the proper programming.

What she should have done was to stay at the office and to ask Harper to place the call. Her paralegal would have made it clear this was a business, not a social, call. Something necessary for the administration of Brunswik.

It wasn't that she wanted to hear his voice again and be reassured he liked their date.

I can call whomever I want, whenever I want, she thought. I am an adult. I am a citizen. I have the constitutional right to call people day or night. If they don't like it, they should unlist their number or cease to communicate electronically. Harold has a lot of nerve not wanting me to call so soon after the date, if I so desire.

Against her better judgment and, only for an instant, taking her eyes off the road, she found the shortcut to Harold's number and pushed the button on her cell phone with resolute bravado.

"Hello?"

"It's Maggie, Harold."

When Harold didn't immediately answer, Maggie wondered if she had shocked him so much he'd had a seizure. Could she just pretend that she'd dialed the wrong number? That wouldn't work. She'd called him by name.

"I bet you didn't expect to hear from me today," she said. Or ever, probably. Dumb start.

"Yes, hello. It's nice to hear your voice. I've been thinking about you. I enjoyed our time together. I was going to call you on Wednesday to see if you were busy this weekend."

Sweet of you. Thanks for dampening down the humiliation, Maggie thought. "I had a good time too." Avoid being sloppy or besotted like a puppy. Honestly, we're both adults. It's not like I'm throwing myself at him. Is it? "I was just talking to Harper and, well, she said something that really caught my attention. I know you aren't following Brunswik news, but she mentioned that you'd talked to Severn Matalokus, that he was a friend of yours." Overstating would bring out the truth quickly.

157

"Yes, I know him, or knew him back when. Dealt with him in constructing a corporate headquarters. What do you want to know about him?"

"He's just gone. He was supposed to build a shopping mall and received all the city approval necessary and licenses, then disappeared and cannot be reached."

"Doesn't sound like him. He was very business-like. Always ready with the details. Dependable. Actually, I wouldn't say we were friends, more like associates. I had a drink or two with him when he came around, and then, at the site, talked sports with him. Oh, sometime later, he gave me two tickets to the Bears game, when he couldn't go himself. Really good seats."

Now I'm making progress, she thought. Matalokus was a Bears fan. An insight that opens up no new passageways. "What was he like? I met him, but I have only my initial impressions."

"I hate to gossip about him, but really, the guy was quite a womanizer."

What, Maggie thought, would that entail? Considering the source, since you've only gone on one date since your wife died? "Really, like what?"

"He was flirting with every woman in the bar. Hitting on them. Not taking no for an answer. Obnoxious. While at the same time, complaining about his wife."

"He's married?" Playing dumb to get more information. "I'm almost sure he told me he was widower. He wasn't wearing a ring. Was this a long time ago when you saw him?" Maybe he'd divorced since then?

"Several years ago. Before I retired. I called him about six months ago. I thought to invite him to go golfing with the boys, but never heard back from him. I know he liked to golf, because he told me that once."

Great, now I know two things for sure, Maggie thought. Matalokus liked the Bears and golf. Maybe he's at the Bears training camp, playing golf.

Chapter Twenty-Eight

Ash's message:

Burn this. I am not writing this report of my criminal activities to you, and if this missive surfaces and there is an attempt to use it against me in a court of law, I will deny I ever wrote this or wrote this under extreme duress, such as a threat against my children. I want a lawyer before I will even tell you my name, much less confess.

You who cannot be named, you who gave me the assignment of breaking and entering into the home of the absent Greek developer, know who you are. I can appreciate your unwillingness to reveal your identity, since it would be a gross violation of the public trust if the mayor of Brunswik were found to have committed such a gross violation.

Firstly, I need to introduce my partner in crime, my co-conspirator with you, the one who should be charged with the same felonies as you or I. Dooley, if you are reading this, you are as guilty as me and the Mayor. Don't deny it. I can tell when you are lying, because the truth is like a foreign language to you.

The Dooley I mean is an anthropology professor at the university that resides, bides, or is situated or located in the City of Brunswik, Illinois. Not living, thankfully, in a State of Missouri. Dooley, who is wise behind his ears. Dooley, who sits upon the ground and beats a drum, cognizant of the hidden truths of human existence. The drum is cognizant, not Dooley.

Let me start at the most logical point. I was born and live. I have good teeth.

You who cannot be named, oh, what the heck, you, Maggie, came over to my office at the university, where I hide between my lectures on logic and statistics, and made a proposal, one that I now regret. I may say I now regret it, but we both know that at the time you made such a proposal, I was already regretting it.

Your question, to melt this proposal down into its constituent parts, was simply this: you wished my humble self, a person of extreme integrity, and my drunken associate, Dooley, to break into the home, the compound, the reservation of one Severn Matalokus. He who has been missing and is presumed not to be present even in his own home, but who may be there and, if he is, may be walled in.

Also, you asked for a reconnoiter of the house, implying that there might be pictures, or photo albums or even a living historian whose job is to await burglars so he can tell them family stories stretching back millennium. Or living relatives, for that matter.

"Dooley," I said, after you left the friendly confines of my office. "Dooley, this way leads to madness. Somehow this worthy woman has formed the impression, who knows how, that you and I are nothing more than common burglars. That, given the opportunity, you and I would actually push through the boundaries set by society and insert ourselves where we should not go."

"Heaven forfend," said Dooley.

As always diligent, I set about to research Severn's home. I was able to secure a property sale listing, such as is distributed by real estate agents to prospective buyers via the Internet, from the time the mansion was most recently purchased, about 10 years prior.

Said listing also had a floor plan. On this basis, I say the house in question was a mansion and still is, because it has so many rooms, and specifically, so many bathrooms. Also there is land around it and it can be seen from a distance.

The mansion is not presently for sale, the first bit of interesting information I am able to supply to you. On the basis of not being for sale, it is my opinion that someone or other is not presently interested in the selling of the property, implying that whoever is still present there wishes to remain there, or, if not there, is not interested in someone else taking up residence there. Being a logician is a burden, no?

The property listing also indicated what school district the mansion was and probably still is in, and its approximate real estate taxes, which even10 years ago, was and is considerably more than my yearly salary, which is none of your business.

On the Internet, I was also able to see pictures of several of the rooms, including the massive "great room," which had been attached electronically to the listing, the pictures not the rooms.

I say "see" because my near-sightedness has been corrected. I have to admit that the great room is a great room, suitable for all purposes, such as huge parties, or, if one is alone, to sit before the fire and think about money.

A family room was also pictured but, unfortunately, did not show or provide an image of the family that presently has lives there, if they do, but also doesn't show the previous tenants.

I can state that, historically, a family room would also have furniture, the kind a family sinks into. Of course, none of this is relevant and was, as we shall see, most likely not the same furniture as was present when the Matalokuses took possession and refurnished.

I must assume that odd pieces of wood and upholstery, as well as sophisticated mechanical systems that allowed for the recline of recliners and such, were brought into the home by the Matalokuses from previous Matalokus residences, or even the residences of Matalokus forebears or those of the previous homes of Mrs. Matalokus, should she exist.

Secondly, I was able to secure a more recent article from a noted architectural magazine, also on the Internet, disappointedly again, not showing the Matalokuses. The mansion, it turns out, was built from the plans of a noted architect and has overhangs and vaulted ceilings and such as mark a residence as being other than a cookie-cutter suburban subdivision, where normal folks live, I am told.

Also in the pictures, I saw what the kitchen looks like when cleaned up by a maid and shown in their best light, using the best lights. This and other rooms so-pictured were obviously designed by interior decorators and no item is allowed to be moved or removed.

Have I told you we observed the Matalokus residence twice, doing our due diligence?

On our first visit, we came by one late afternoon and confirmed the reports you had provided that someone comes out of an internal, subterranean garage each day in a darkened limo and returns the same way. We did not actually see the limo come out, but assume that, once upon a time, it must have come out or we could not have observed it presently, as it came back in.

We also observed that the limo driver, presumably who possesses a limo driver's license, leaves after delivering someone or no one, and returns, most likely, each weekday morning to restart the ritual.

We could follow him, if you so desire, but this is a separate assignment, beyond the scope of your current charge.

But to continue my narrative, Dooley and I went the second time, in the middle of the night, and stood a distance from the mansion and simply looked at it.

"Looks like any house of very wealthy people," Dooley observed.

"Ah, but it does have a few structural elements that might be considered conventional," I pointed out. "It has a front door and windows. Each window has a window treatment. When the window treatment is withdrawn, or raised or removed, someone can look both from the outside into the mansion and from the inside, can look to the outside."

"Well and good," he said. "A thought: such homes have alarms."

"True and turning off the power from the outside will just bring someone out from the security firm to check. Moreover, doing so, by, for instance, snapping all incoming electrical lines, if we knew how to do that, might disturb the residents, even if they are asleep. To explain, it has happened to me during power outages, the mere lack of

house sounds, such as air conditioning, can be so disturbing it can force me from a deep sleep."

"I think," Dooley said, "that, at best, we can hope for about 10 minutes inside before someone, such as a policeman, arrives to investigate. I think we should enter at a point that would be far from bedrooms to maximize our time before discovery."

We formed a plan. I would break a window at the rear of the house. Then, we, our faces darkened with the same stuff they put under the eyes of football players to reduce glare but in this case to hide our identities, would run like hell through the house and back out again, checking every room and gathering whatever personal items seemed most revelatory. Much like fraternity boys on a scavenger hunt, the basic experience upon which we built our expertise.

Pursuant to said plan, I did break a rear window, pushed it open, and, followed by Dooley, ran inside. We checked each room and the basement, unfortunately finding no person. I saw no wall that looked like it had recently been rebricked with a body therein. Having thought to bring a bag with us, I stole whatever pictures were there and also what I thought was a family album and any family memorabilia or things that looked old.

In our search and investigation, Dooley, being much less agile and graceful than myself, was so clumsy that anyone present but hiding would have immediately come from wherever he or she was secretly lurking to see who was looting their manor, or the manner of someone's looting.

I must confess now one of my major regrets, not of our illegal intrusion which I enjoyed, but that I forgot to check the inside of the freezer in the basement. This freezer was the kind that lies on its back with the door on top. The user needs to open the door, prop it up and move the frozen bodies of relatives who are not yet buried, so that one can retrieve some ice cream, as necessary, to elegantly entertain guests.

Should my mother in law, Louise, so die and her death could so be hidden, I would consider placing her *body in such permanent deep freeze to allay funeral costs. However, I suppose, Suzanne would object.*

In any case, I had run out of time, so I did not check the contents of the freezer, but ran with Dooley, out the way we came. Thus, I could not testify in a court of law that no one was frozen in the freezer. I am sorry about this exception to my investigation, and, if necessary, would stipulate to the non-existence of such body. Unless, you want to believe that such body is there and want me to stipulate the opposite.

I have the attached personal items for your inspection and for whatever conclusions you may reach.

Chapter Twenty-Nine

Article by Becky:

Brunswik Mayor Maggie Wellington has been endorsed by the Democratic Party to replace the late State Representative Raul Markham, (D-30th) who died early Sunday morning.

Governor Del Essen is expected to appoint Mayor Wellington Friday to fill the vacated seat. Mayor Wellington will face election with full party support in November of next year and is considered the favorite for election.

At a press conference this morning, Mayor Wellington, who has served for almost nine years and been elected to three terms as mayor of the prominent suburb, welcomed the party endorsement and said she looked forward to meeting with state officials, prior to the official appointment.

"The Governor, Lt. Governor, State Senate leadership, and the Speaker of the House will meet with me in Springfield at the end of the week. Although I do not have an agenda for the meeting, I am assured that the meeting is pro forma and will be a discussion of the appointment and campaign issues.

"I am, of course, thrilled and humbled by the opportunity to serve the North Shore community in a more comprehensive manner, and I hope to meet with key constituents as soon as possible."

In his statement of his intention to appoint Mrs. Wellington, Governor Essen emphasized the Mayor's experience in government, her growing popularity in her role as Mayor of one of the "jewels of the North Shore", and her strong support from within party.

Margaret Philapaitis Wellington is a long-time Brunswik resident and made her name as a lawyer in high profile custody cases and in advocating on educational issues for handicapped children.

She is a native of Chicago and is the widow of a prominent businessman. She served on multiple Brunswik city committees before serving as an alderman, and later, as Mayor.

Mrs. Wellington has two daughters and two grandchildren.

In a side-bar, with the headline, "Who Will Replace Mayor Wellington?":

Conjecture has begun almost immediately about who will fill out the term of Mayor Wellington, following her appointment, expected late Friday night.

Speculation is divided because so little time has passed since the unfortunate arson death of the late Alderman Gene Casey, who had often been mentioned as a possible successor to Mayor Wellington. Police are following leads and expect to have a press conference soon to report progress in the investigation, according to Brunswik Police Chief Feather.

It is believed that Brunswik City Council Alderman Merit Berger, who has been the most vocal critic of Mayor Wellington's administration, may consider seeking the party endorsement for Mayor. Alternatively, other candidates, some of whom have been mentioned in the past as possible successors of Senator Markham might also receive the party backing, to avoid a costly primary battle for the state office.

Because the mayoralty is non-partisan by law, less is known about possible candidates on the conservative spectrum. Some local businessmen have also voiced interest in the past about serving in the city government and might throw their hats into the ring.

"Even an idiot knows," Maggie said, "that the Governor and the others are going to demand I come out against the mall project, before they sign on to my appointment. Why the mall project is the focus of so much, I can only imagine, but the simplest, therefore the best, answer is that the Governor and every state official will somehow take a financial hit if the project is ever completed."

Harper nodded and simultaneously shrugged, to indicate she agreed and also had no idea how to respond. The office phone rang on Harper's desk and she ran out of the Maggie's office to answer the call. "It's Mr. Wally," she called out to Maggie. "I have my hand over the receiver. What do you want me to tell him to do?"

Unladylike suggestions crossed Maggie's mind. "Tell him I'll call him back."

"Mrs. Wellington is in conference," Harper said into the phone. "Do you want to leave a message?" Harper paused for a reply. Wally's bark was just slightly below an audible level for Maggie, but loud enough for Harper to take the phone away from ear in self-protection. Harper wrote down some of the details of Mr. Wally's monologue.

He must have broken the connection because Harper replaced the phone on the receiver and told Maggie, "He says he will schedule your flight for Friday and will be traveling to Springfield with you."

Sitting with Mr. Wally for even an hour will drive me insane, Maggie thought. More insane.

Harper continued. "I've written down the flight number. Mr. Wally is working on an acceptance speech and asks that you review the faces of the state officials from pictures on the Internet. Just a thought: If you're going to Springfield instead of into hiding, I'll have to clear off Friday from your calendar."

"You do that. In the meantime, I'll be unavailable for the next two hours."

Sitting in Suzanne's office, Maggie spread out the booty from Ash and Dooley's jaunt through the Matalokus mansion. "I'm conveniently not telling you when I received these. I'm also not telling you one way or another whether these have been stolen. Assume I have inherited them or that they are lost objects I found under a tree."

Suzanne didn't think she needed to reply, so didn't. Her patient was speaking and that was sufficient. No need to prime Maggie's verbal pump.

In front of them was a picture of Severn Matalokus, probably, at age seven or so. Also pictured was a very similar looking child, but slightly smaller and younger, apparently the other Matalokus brother, Anthony. Between them was a large man with a huge black mustache, every inch the immigrant progenitor of the American wing of the Matalokus family.

"What do you make of this?" Maggie asked.

"I think," Suzanne said, "from the children's clothes and the backdrop, which appears to be a mountain scene, that we're looking at one of those pictures taken at a department store in the 50's, say, just past the mid-50's. The boys are separated by their father, who is smiling bravely. He looks like he has just kept the boys from doing physical harm to each other. Both boys have their eyebrows raised and possibly, like cats, their backs arched for the attack."

"That's consistent with what I was told. That the boys didn't get along."

"Also, the father is inclining his head towards one of the boys. This might indicate some favoritism or some extra attention of some sort in regard to the slightly smaller of the two. Maybe he was being protective."

Maggie nodded, but did not want to slow the observations with her comments.

Suzanne's dutifully continued. "The two boys couldn't be more than a year and a half or two years apart, so maybe their ages are seven and nine. There's such a strong family resemblance, the one boy differing from the other only by height. I suppose that both of them strongly resemble their father."

Maggie said, "I think I can see Severn Matalokus' mature face in his father's. Except for the mustache, and, of course, the Severn I saw was much older than the man in this picture."

"What else have you?" Suzanne asked. Pointing, "Is this some kind of family album?"

"Yes. I feel very guilty about this. Or I would if I had anything to do with the mysterious appearance of this album. Stealing precious family pictures is both a social and criminal act. But to analyze what we have, the album appears to be from early in Severn's marriage. Many informal pictures, possibly from the honeymoon. It's not always easy to see the older person in the younger person's picture, but I'd say this was probably the woman I saw at the City Council meeting that approved Severn's mall project."

"So," Suzanne said, "you're theorizing that this is Severn's wife and that she still is living these days because you saw her."

"Yes I saw her at a restaurant on Saturday night."

Suzanne is probably thinking I see this woman everywhere, Maggie thought. She's probably concluded that I'm so fixated on Severn that I'm making up a story about his wife. "I see. Did you talk to her?"

"I was on a triple date and we were all walking out as this woman walked in. I was embarrassed about stopping everyone so I could talk or hanging back and ignoring my date." Besides, Maggie told herself, I couldn't remember the woman's name.

Suzanne brightened. "What about this date? I may need to report this to a higher power. My mother."

"I don't know how I feel about Harold. But I'm beginning to place him more towards the normal category, as opposed to just about every other man I've met in the last week."

"Do you think you'll go on a second date?"

"I think my impetuous call to him makes that a certainty. I should be back from Springfield by early Saturday morning, so I could go out Saturday night."

"Right. But to get back to recent events, I haven't properly congratulated you. Imagine, being a State Senator and I knew you when."

Still a little premature to say that, Maggie thought. I still must meet with the higher ups and pledge my undying loyalty, thereby forever compromising my integrity. "Thanks, yes. I'm thrilled."

"Are you done then with the Matalokus investigation? Or do you think this Mrs. Matalokus is following you about?"

She's asking if my paranoia has reached stage 2, or whatever is the stage where the patient goes over the edge. "No, but it's possible she has taken up residence in Brunswik. It was the impression of those who I don't know who might have invaded the Matalokus mansion, that no one lives there."

"I see," Suzanne said, probably making a mental note to put this weird reply, word for word, in the file she'd created for Maggie.

"I suppose I should tell you that I will be asking those who I don't know to get in touch with the Matalokus chauffeur."

"I'm sure that will make the frat brothers very happy."

Chapter Thirty

Press Release from City Hall on Wednesday morning:

Mayor Wellington has added another agenda item for Thursday night's regular meeting of the Brunswik City Council. The council will take up the question of whether the proposed shopping mall should be revived with some other developer or if the project should be rejected and city approval withdrawn.

Mayor Wellington has invited all interested parties to attend the meeting. Time for comments from the floor has been allotted. A statement will be read from the city Plan Commission, with its recommendation.

Anyone can attend the open part of the meeting, but a council discussion in closed session is possible after all the information is gathered. A vote might be made publicly after the Council returns to open session.

Any interested party who wishes to submit written comment should provide such to the City Clerk, with adequate time to make copies for the alderman and city officials.

The project was approved by the Council last June. However, the developer has indicated, through his inaction, his inability to perform. A representative of the developer, Matalokus Holdings, has declined to appear at the meeting.

Report from Becky:

A prominent North Shore businessman and philanthropist, Oswalt Michaels, 92, was found murdered late Wednesday night in the office of his estate.

Michaels, who traced his family back to the pioneer days of the North Shore and who may have been its wealthiest resident based on his real estate holdings, was found on the floor of his study by an associate.

Police said that Michaels had been dead for some time when found. No effort was made to resuscitate him, and he was pronounced dead on arrival at the Brunswik Hospital. His cause of death will be established by the Cook County Coroner's office but apparently was a gunshot to the chest.

Sources who asked not to be named say police are baffled how an assailant could have entered Michaels' mansion and private office without being seen by security guards. Michaels was known to be obsessed with his privacy and had multiple cameras focused around the estate and its entrance.

Police have examined recordings from the security cameras but apparently have had no success in identifying an intruder.

The near impossibility of gaining access from the outside has focused police investigation regarding those who were known to be in the mansion around the time of Michaels' death, at approximately 8 p.m. His body was discovered at almost midnight.

No appointments were scheduled for the early evening, and it is unknown specifically why Michaels would be in his office. However, such activity was not unusual, according to staff members, who asked not to be identified. Michaels often sat alone in his office at night, when unable to sleep.

At least 10 employees of the estate were present in the mansion at the probable time of the murder, and local police have asked for extra help from neighboring departments to interview each.

Michael's heir is most likely his son, Stewart, who is in his late 60's and who lives in New Mexico, in retirement. He has been notified and is returning to the North Shore, sources indicated.

"Michaels probably had many enemies, starting with the Algonquin tribe and Jefferson Davis," Maggie said, "but the murder of a man that old must be some kind of message." She and Detective Smith sat in Maggie's law office.

"You are kidding, of course," Detective Smith said, "except for the message part."

"Yes, and the message was meant for me, but to do what? Let's come back to that question. My mind is going in all directions this morning. You arrived at the Michaels mansion when?"

"This morning. I interviewed a few of the domestic help. Besides hating Michaels and having no fear of speaking ill of the dead, they did not know anyone who specifically wanted to kill Michaels right now. According to one employee, the quote 'nasty bastard' unquote, deserved anything he got. That kind of statement must be taken seriously when it can be used against the speaker in a court of law, as the mantra goes."

"What's your feeling about it, professionally speaking?" Maggie asked.

"If you're asking what I'm guessing, separate from the actual determinable facts, someone inside the mansion decided to off Mr. Michaels, then escaped in the tumult afterwards. In other words, he was already in the mansion, didn't come in from outside or he'd have been observed, and didn't flee the scene as the first policemen assumed, but hung around and left at his convenience."

"Which means what, profile-wise?"

"First that the murderer didn't look like anyone's idea of a murderer, slack-jawed and drooling. To the employees, he looked like someone with the police and to the police, he looked like an employee. He probably had good nerves if he could appear calm when he emerged from his hiding place and walked out with those investigating the crime."

"What else did you learn about the murder?"

Smith swiveled in his chair. "No one paid much attention to the physical condition of remote areas within the mansion. I took it upon myself to look at each room.

173

I found two doors that looked like they had been forced at some time in the past. Forced from the inside. As if the doors had been locked, and someone who wanted to get out was able to push the door open by breaking the lock, without doing too much damage to the surrounding masonry. These locks must have been constructed by Paul Revere."

Most likely, Maggie thought. "So the murderer was ordinary looking, not prepossessing, and may have been held prisoner in the mansion for some time. He was brought in when no one was taking notice and escaped by just looking officious, therefore invisible."

"That's what I'm saying."

Well, now we know what Rauptt has been up to, Maggie thought. "To change the subject again, what's happening with the investigation into the Alderman Casey murder/arson case

"Nothing is happening except for waiting until the investigation is old news so it can be forgotten. The articles said that a news conference would be held, which I think is very unlikely. Chief Feather isn't going to greet newspeople with a load of 'I don't knows.'"

Maggie stacked papers on the desktop into a neat pile. She hated a messy desk. "Were you able to find anything more about Mrs. Matalokus?"

"She exists or did exist, is all. I did discover that their residence is in her name. Which isn't all that suspicious, considering that developers are always worried that the corporate veil will be pierced and they'll be held personally liable for debts. Losing everything, including their homes and personal property."

"It's still suspicious," Maggie said, "that nothing else exists about the wife. This lady never did anything? Never joined the local horticulture society, didn't entertain, wasn't mentioned as an organizer of events? Stuff that rich women do, who aren't specifically doing anything?"

"Right. She was apparently keeping a very low profile. Had no children."

Maggie shifted in her chair. "Having no kids would mean she was probably very focused on her husband. But if that were true, she would have demanded police action if her husband really had disappeared."

"I suppose."

"Were you ever able to find out about property transfers for the real estate around the proposed mall?" she asked.

"There was a flurry of activity about two years ago, when I assume properties changed hands before the project was announced. Here's something that may or may not be interesting. Titles to the properties have changed hands within the last six months from one blind trust to another."

"That's another fact I can't interpret," Maggie said. "I need to think this whole thing through. See everything as part of everything else. If you don't mind, I'll think out loud and you stop me if what I say makes no sense."

"Go."

"Someone wanted the project to proceed, so burned down the present mall, as best he could. Which makes some sense. Like it's too late now, the city needs to do something with the property, so let's continue the project. I didn't see this right away because Alderman Casey was killed, and he was for the project. Killing him was anti-project."

"And now you think differently?"

"Yes, maybe there was a separate reason to kill Casey. Maybe he was blackmailing whoever killed him."

"I always like blackmail as a motive." Smith said.

"When it looked like the project would be revived because the orphaned businesses needed some place to go, pressure was brought on me to kill the project by bribing me with a state senator appointment. When it looked like that might not sway me, those against the project reciprocated by kidnapping the chairperson of the planning commission, Rauptt, the only one with the expertise to continue the project."

175

"Right, Rauptt was in favor of the project. Makes some sense. Then what?"

"The announcement was made that I would be appointed State Senator. Except that the appointment wouldn't be official until I capitulated and came out against the project. So I capitulated and I decided to steer a council meeting towards rejection of the project. Why not? I wanted to be done with it and because part of me still wants to be state senator, loss of integrity or not. Also, I wanted to see what would happen. I hope I'm not disillusioning you about politics or politicians."

"I don't think it's possible to lower my opinion. But to get back to your meeting, that was an anti-project move? So it was time for a hit back by those in favor of the project?"

"Yes, I hoped I'd hear more directly from the pro-project people, but I didn't anticipate that the pro-project people would act so quickly by murdering Michaels. In other words, his murder was a hit back by the pro-project people."

"So under your, you hit me, I'll hit you, theory, what happens next?"

"Now that Michaels has been murdered, so can't take revenge on me, neither the pro or the con side can be sure what I'll do at the meeting."

"Not sure how that follows."

"I look like one thing to the pro-people and like another person to the anti-people The anti-group fears I'm not intimidated anymore because Michaels is dead and I'll manipulate the council to continue to complete the project. The pro-group is worried I didn't get the message from Michael's death, that I'm still intimidated by the anti-group, and that I will sabotage the project at the council meeting."

"If you say so. What's next?"

Chapter Thirty-One

The ring of the telephone woke Maggie from a profound sleep. Her first thought was that her mother was in trouble, ill or dying. Belatedly, she remembered her mother was already dead. Her next thought was to have her husband answer the phone. She felt over to his side of the bed to give him a nudge. He, however, was also dead.

"Yes, yes, what's wrong?" she said into the phone near her bed. Thoughts of other horrors--car accidents, heart attacks and aneurysms, poisonings, explosions-- swept her brain.

"Mother, it's Kim." The voice straining. Was this a middle of the night attempt to reconcile with her mother? Surely, her daughter could have waited to have her catharsis at a more civilized time of day. "It's Ethan! Someone has snatched him. We thought he'd gone to a neighbor's house. We got this odd call. He's been kidnapped. I'm so frightened!"

Maggie looked at her clock. She'd fallen asleep as soon as her head hit her pillow, just, supposedly, a short nap after dinner. It was only 9 p.m., but she'd thought it was the middle of the night.

Maggie experienced an unbearable desire to hug her daughter and to make everything right. She needed to go immediately to Kim, share her grief, and to try to help. "I'll be there in a few moments. Hold on. Maybe it's all a mistake, and he was invited to dinner and forgot to tell you? Have you called the police?"

"No, the man on the phone told me not to. I can't think! I don't know what to do."

"I'm on my way."

Still in her clothes, Maggie jumped from bed. Taking her car keys off a hook in the kitchen while in mid-run, she was out the door in record time. As the elevator descended loudly, she suppressed her urge to analyze. In the underground garage, she opened the car door and leaped into the front seat.

No longer able to stop the scary thoughts: her grandson was in danger. Who would do such a thing?

Maggie had a sudden realization. In her recounting to Smith the events surrounding the mall project, she'd left out the part where Ethan had fallen from a slide and broken his arm. Kim had been very hazy about why the fall happened, and Maggie wondered, for the first time, whether or not Kim had really witnessed the accident. Maybe Ethan's fall hadn't just been a case of a momentary loss of balance. What if his injury had been another message.

Surroundings blurred. Night had fully descended. Maggie thought she heard a new rattle in the car's engine. Hopefully the car wouldn't stall when she needed it the most. If she was stopped for speeding, at least being Mayor would preclude a ticket.

Maggie ran up the walk to Kim's house. Kim was already at the screen door and swung it open as her mother approached.

Immediately Maggie and Kim hugged. Maggie hoped she wasn't squeezing the breath out of Kim.

"I'm so frightened," Kim repeated.

Kim's husband, Brad, stood behind Kim, realizing that his wife needed comforting from her mother, not logical alternatives from a, focused-on-one-thing-at-a-time, man.

"Tell me about it. Ethan was where, the last time you saw him?"

Kim: "He went off with his best friend, Jacob, just down the street, like almost every day. Ethan promised to come home in time for dinner. He and Jacob were going to play in Jacob's yard. Jacob had his birthday recently and had some new toys. Ethan said he'd be careful about his arm."

"I had a thought while driving up. Kim, tell the truth, where were you with Ethan when he fell from the slide and broke his arm? Were your eyes on him?"

Kim reacted as if she'd been hit in the face with the accusation that she was a bad mother. "I wasn't far. I was chasing the baby. My eyes were off Ethan for a second. There were other mothers in the park."

"Did he say he'd been pushed off the slide?"

"He made all kinds of excuses. That he lost his balance. That the boy behind him gave him a push. Why? Is this important?"

"I don't think this kidnapping is the first time someone has tried to hurt or scare Ethan."

"Mother, is this something about you? You always turn everything into something about you. Are you saying that someone has a grudge against you and took it out on Ethan?"

Maggie couldn't think of an answer that wouldn't antagonize her daughter. Kim took Maggie's silence as a "yes."

"Oh mother, is this your damn politics again? You just have to be in the public eye where you're a great big target. And now it's involved even an innocent child."

Thankfully, Maggie's answer was swallowed in her throat when Tracy and James came through the screen door. Tracy immediately hugged Kim, whispering reassurances. James moved over to stand near Brad, in the "better keep quiet" zone.

Done hugging her sister, Tracy moved to comfort her mother. "This will be alright. I'm sure no one would hurt Ethan."

I raised a somewhat naive child, Maggie thought. Tracy was, though, probably right, at least for the moment. This wasn't a matter of hurting someone as an expression of some mania, but something purposeful, to bring the maximum pressure on Maggie.

"Let's sit around the table," Maggie said. "Maybe we can come to some course of action if we pool our resources."

179

Each person present sat at the long dining room table. The daughters automatically took the seats in their traditional positions, one on either side of Maggie, who sat at what could have been the foot of the table. Their father and her husband had always sat facing Maggie, from the position at the head of the table, as patriarch.

The men sat near their respective mates, neither daring to take the patriarch position, or just not wanting to face their mother-in-law or future MIL.

Maggie looked at them all one by one. Her family, but one was missing and the other asleep.

"What exactly did this man say on the phone? It was a man wasn't it? I think you said that."

"Yes, a man," Kim said.

"Was he smooth and boastful or kind of reserved?" Maggie wanted to know if the call had come from Mr. Wally or from Rauptt. She had settled on these two as representatives of the opposing sides in the chess match.

"It was a he and he called about an hour ago, just as we hung up the phone after talking with Jacob's parents. They'd sent Ethan down the block to go home for dinner just like usual. Ethan never made it home. Someone must have snatched him on the street. Here in a safe neighborhood with so many eyes watching. Where I will never feel safe again, and I'll never be able to relax when the children aren't right under my nose."

Attempting to get her back on track, Maggie asked, "How did his voice sound, anxious, emotional?"

"Deathly calm. Icy. Determined"

"Did he ask for a ransom?" Maggie asked. Any amount of money wouldn't equal a fraction of what Ethan's love was worth.

"No, and that's what was even more frightening. He said . . ."

"Exact words, if possible," Maggie said.

"He started 'Is this Ethan's mother?' I hoped for a moment that this was some parent down the street who'd found Ethan playing with the family puppy. My puppy playing with an actual puppy."

180

Maggie started to feel annoyance that Kim couldn't just tell her what was said.

"I said 'yes, where is he? Is he alright? Put him on the phone.' The man said 'Don't worry. We have no intention of hurting him. He's safe as long as you don't call the police.'"

Interrupting despite her desire to hear the whole conversation, Maggie asked, "He said 'we'?"

"Yes."

It takes two to conspire, Maggie thought. Rauptt and Mrs. Matalokus? She'd been literally in the picture that she saw at Rauptt's condo. What was their connection? Ex wife? Sister?

Kim went on. "The man said, 'You know why I'm doing this.' Not a question, but as if I knew of some reason. I think I said, 'What in the world are you talking about'?'"

Or was it Mr. Wally and Edelton the aide to the Speaker? Taking this opportunity to gain complete control over Maggie, forcing her to nix the project by putting Ethan in danger.

"Then what did he say?" Maggie asked.

"There was a pause as if he had put his hand over the receiver, like he was getting more instructions. I shouted into the phone that I wanted to talk to Ethan, which must have interrupted the side conversation. The next thing I heard was Ethan saying, "I'm alright mom. Please don't be mad at me.' That little voice of his when he thinks he's been caught doing something wrong. Also, "They said they would take me home as soon as Ya-Ya does what she's promised.'"

Kim gave her mother an incensed look. "What did you promise?"

Had she made some promise? She didn't remember making any. She'd studiously avoided promises. She'd avoided any statement on the subject of the mall project each time some lunatic wanted to know her position.

As for her promising her support for the mall project, she hadn't even voted on it, hadn't needed to break a council tie because the vote was unanimous. She'd said little at that meeting. The council had just followed a routine recommendation of the Planning commission.

"Then what?" Maggie asked.

"Something must have startled them, because I heard an abrupt hang-up."

Was the other side, whichever that was, breaking down the door?

Chapter Thirty-Two

"I demand the return of my cell phone," Mr. Wally said. This being the equivalent of an elephant wanting his tusks back, a raptor wanting back his talons and flesh tearing beak, a bee its stinger, a wolf its serrated teeth in a massive jaw.

Maggie observed behind a one-way mirror. Earlier this morning, Smith's uncle, the Chief of Police of the suburb where Mr. Wally resided, had detained the political operative for questioning in connection with his failure to renew his auto plates by two days and for insulting police in a manner that could be broadly interpreted as interfering with a police investigation.

Smith and his Uncle Pop were being patient. "When you could have been over at the department of motor vehicles getting your plates renewed, you were where, instead, yesterday?"

Mr. Wally straightened to his full sitting height. "I know this is some kind of political retribution. Know this. No public employee intimidates Mr. Wally. It's Mr. Wally who intimidates the public employee, with the full support of the entire political pantheon. You two are in big, big, big trouble. Besides, I don't have time to play with you boys. I'm going to see the governor tomorrow."

"Just be patient and answer a few questions," Pop said.

"You guys are transparent. You've got me trapped here and are afraid to tell me the real reason. You'll have to spell it out once my lawyer arrives or you'll just have to let me go."

Pop wasn't his real first name, just what Smith chose to call him to be consistent with what his children called him. He was a very tall, overweight man, with a prominent stomach hanging on a frame of steel. "Don't

183

worry about a charge," Uncle Pop said. "Lack of cooperation is enough to hold you."

"For not answering fast enough why I missed the deadline for an auto license sticker? All that was required was a $150 ticket, which I would have paid gladly. You guys are going to be really embarrassed when I sue you for false arrest."

"You aren't under arrest," Uncle Pop said. "But I advise you to talk to us. We just need to clear up a few matters. Then we'll just forget your initial show of resistance and insults to our officers."

"I'm about to cease my cooperation and walk out."

"Best to answer a few questions," Smith said.

Temporarily resigned. "Never let it be said that Mr. Wally doesn't cooperate with our boys in blue."

"Where were you all of yesterday, starting with getting up in the morning until the time you were brought in by police?"

"Yesterday? Was a day like any other. I rose. I kissed my wife and children. I ate breakfast. I called my office to get my messages. I went into my study and I called everyone back. That took over an hour. I got dressed and drove downtown to my office. I took phone calls. I conferred with those I advise on political matters. I gathered political intelligence."

You mean gossip, Maggie thought.

"What did you do last night?" Uncle Pop asked.

"I stayed until 8 p.m. at the office. You can check with my secretary. I ate at a local restaurant downtown. I'm a regular there, and you can ask them. You can check my credit card. I used it at the restaurant. After that, I returned to the office and wrote Mayor Wellington's statement for after she is appointed on Friday, thanking the governor profusely. I stayed at my office until 10:30. My secretary was not there when I left, but I did sign out of the building. I then went to the parking lot where I keep my car, and used my credit card again. In the time it always takes to go home, I got home."

That was a pretty good story, documented by records. Maggie wondered if that wasn't the point, being able to account for his time. "You didn't, I suppose, borrow someone else's car during the day or take the train home and come back to your office later?" Pop asked.

"No, and did I have someone else sit at my desk making phone calls you can check. Did I have my secretary dress up like me and lower her voice? What is this, some kind of police harassment? This isn't a police state, yet."

Ignoring his sarcasm. "At no time did you drive to Brunswik yesterday?"

"Drive to Brunswik? Why should I? To consult with Mayor Wellington? There was no need. If I wanted to talk to her, I would have just called her. She would have, of course, immediately take my call. I am liaisoning for her during this interim before she becomes State Senator."

"You did not talk to or see Mrs. Wellington's grandchild?" Smith asked.

Mr. Wally started to speak, then shut his mouth. He'd done a better job of interrogating his interrogators than they of him.

The creation of pathways between nerve fibers in his brain was almost audible as he digested the gossip that something had happened to Maggie's grandson. He decided who was the first person he would call and how this matter affected the whole amorphic, ever changing, ball of wax that was politics in the State of Illinois.

Smith continued to ask questions, but Pop stood up heavily, exited the room, and sat down next to Maggie. Both watched Smith in action for a while. "That boy, who is like a son to me, will go far," Pop said. "Don't you agree?"

"Definitely. I need to express my thanks to you and Detective Smith for keeping a lid on the kidnapping. If I'd gone to the Brunswik police, I would be hearing the whole story on television in the morning news."

185

"That's perfectly alright. It's our honor to be trusted by you with this."

She could reward Pop with only a smile. "What do you think of Mr. Wally? Is he telling the truth?

Pop considered and scratched the side of his face in thought. "Yes, I think he is telling the truth. He's not violent. It's just that his head is filled with crap. Excuse my language. Crap about politics and politicians. He's just some kind of political creature. Maybe it would be better to describe him as a political animal in his natural habitat. Lives and breathes politics. He doesn't have a principle or opinion that isn't based in his own self-interest."

"That's how I see him, too. You don't think he's involved in snatching Ethan at all?" Maggie felt confidence when she talked to Pop. He was the voice of experience. "He's been pressuring me to take a certain political position for some time."

"I'm sure he can think of many other ways of making you miserable, like ruining your political career, besides kidnapping your grandson. Politicians are crooked, but usually in a white collar kind of way. They don't want to get involved with the Feds for kidnapping. It's the only good thing about the Federal government. Politicians don't kidnap. And they don't kill each other. That's what separates America from banana republics."

"I hope you're right. I really hope you are."

"Besides, we collected on favors by having the Chicago police check out his office downtown. Mr. Wally didn't leave a squibble or a scratch that indicated an abduction. We checked all his calls yesterday, and he made many fewer than he is letting on. He isn't that important, just thinks he's is. Nobody he called specializes in kidnapping or is known to use those tactics."

When Maggie said nothing, he went on. "We couldn't get a warrant to search his house without revealing the reason, and, in any case, even Mr. Wally wouldn't be stupid enough to stash your grandson in his own house. That would be too close to implicating

186

himself and his family. We did do some checking to see if any neighbor of Wally saw your grandchild, and got nothing. We would have if there had been any kind of ruckus. His house is pretty close to the homes of his neighbors. No extra child and no screaming."

An image of a screaming Ethan crossed her mind and was rejected with some internal fury. Just to hear herself speak, she thought out loud. "The council meeting is tonight. Someone needs to exert maximum pressure on me and has found my weakest spot, my family. It's all about pressure, not ransom. If I do whatever in the world the kidnapper wants me to do at the meeting, I feel confident that Ethan will be returned unharmed. I just don't know what I'm supposed to do."

"Can't you just table the motion for further consideration at the next council meeting? That's what we do in this suburb, and we never actually decide to do anything."

"I'm just worried that the kidnapper will keep Ethan until the next meeting. That wouldn't solve my problem." Pop nodded in silent agreement. "Are you going to let Mr. Wally out, now that you've interrogated him?"

"Yes," Pop said. "We'll tell him, before he's released, that if he even mutters the word 'kidnap' to any of his cronies, we'll grab him back here on suspicion and never let him out. When he hits the streets, we'll watch his every move. A man like that couldn't resist checking on the situation if he's behind the kidnapping. We'll know who he calls."

Maggie's growing anxiety wasn't relieved and her mind continued to churn.

She came to the conclusion that Mr. Wally had not personally snatched her grandchild. She also doubted that he had the guts to be involved in something so illegal. Besides, in the last analysis, Mr. Wally had already succeeded in intimidating her into opposing the project by means of a political bribe. Why would he need to act further?

187

Maggie decided that the kidnappers must be working for Rauptt.

If he killed Michaels, as she suspected, he was capable of anything.

Where was Rauptt?

Chapter Thirty-Three

"It was good of you to come over to my law office," Maggie told Chief Feather. "There's something I need to ask, and I hope you can keep this as confidential as you can, not even mention it to your wonderful wife. I need a favor."

"I'm listening," Chief Feather said.

Instead of the expected leaning forward, he moved his chair a little further back from her desk. An avoidance gesture, Maggie thought. Avoiding the favor or avoiding herself? No one likes to think that someone else is just plain revolted to be in their presence, she thought. Does he hate me that much, or is it all about women in authority?

Push on, Maggie. "I need a gun."

Shock crossed Feather's face. "Why?"

"I've received a lot of feedback on this mall project, some of it downright threatening. I want to be able to defend myself. I know how to shoot a gun. My late husband taught me after a robbery in our neighborhood. I'm not a bad shot. I just don't keep a gun because I hate them."

"I could push through a license pretty fast, but it would be easier if I just swear you in as a deputy."

"I'm willing."

"Raise your right hand." She did and he did the same.

He gave her the traditional oath and she said "I will."

Was there a glint of new respect in Feather's eyes? "I'll be back with a service revolver. Please don't shoot anyone unless it's absolutely necessary. I'll have someone watch your car all day and beef up security for

189

the council meeting tonight. Keep me informed throughout the day about your whereabouts."

A new friendliness, Maggie though. It's like I've joined the fraternity of gun lovers.

"Maggie, I'm just calling to firm up our plans for Saturday night," Harold said. Maggie's hands were still trembling a little from her exchange with Feather. The gun hadn't arrived yet.

Should she tell him that the chances of this date actually happening were declining by the minute?

"Harold, how are you?" She hadn't given Harold much thought since Ethan's abduction and found the transition to her social life a difficult change. She hoped her voice did not reveal her mental state.

"I'm fine. You don't sound so fine."

"Lots of issues. Children in trees, dogs locked in bathrooms, unable to get out." That pretty much summed up the situation without actually telling him what really bothered her.

"I was thinking that I would pick you up from your condo. We could go to this old world Greek restaurant, Mykonis. There's entertainment. We could just sit and talk. No need to load it up with activities, unless you also want to see a movie."

Maggie knew the restaurant. She and her late husband had gone there often. Some of the older employees might recognize her, ask her how she was. Lousy, she would say. Embarrassed to be there with someone besides her still beloved. As if she were being unfaithful.

On the other hand, she thought, life is for the living. It would be such fun to see how the place had changed. The charming owner must be gone by now, in retirement or passed on. The place could be run by his son, also charming, who she'd met a few times.

"Yes, that sounds lovely. Alright, 7:30 would be a good time to pick me up." If I survive the council meeting and meeting with the Governor, and am still in the land of the living. "Do you want me to make reservations?"

190

Grateful. "Yes, thank you."

Harper walked into Maggie's office. Uncharacteristically, she sat on the chair facing her desk. Harper's usual amused tone had morphed into seriousness. "I need to talk to you about something."

At least, it couldn't be about my grandson, Maggie thought. She hadn't told Harper anything about it. No need to upset her too.

Maggie saved the brief she was writing in two or three clicks, then pushed the computer away. This must be something important, Maggie thought, Harper wouldn't have sounded so tentative, unless she was worried about Maggie's reaction.

Why does Harper think she is about to upset me? Too late. I'm already totally upset enough.

"I wanted to bring you up to date about my interview downtown. I'm still in shock. I've never been treated so well and so sought after. I was treated like I was a precious natural resource, a diamond mine that was suddenly on the market. Like a whole world of lawyers woke up one morning and wanted to know what they could do for me."

"Kind of like being seduced?" Maggie asked.

"Exactly. That was the very word that floated through my mind. Like I'd suddenly become the most popular girl in class. Like men were fighting each other for the right and privilege to escort me to the prom."

"Nice. What exactly are they offering?"

"Start now as a clerk with the understanding that I would become an associate as soon as I passed the bar and be put on the fast track to partnership. Honestly, if this weren't happening, I would swear that I'm delusional."

"That's quite an offer. What are you going to do?"

"I don't know what I'm going to do. I'm wondering if this is some kind of deal with the devil. I'm suspicious. I want to know exactly what I'm giving up to get this job. Is it my personal integrity?" Harper lowered her voice even further. "Or would I be giving up control over my life, my destiny, even over my physical self. Would I be asked to do things, you know, with my soul, my body and my sexuality that would conflict forever with my inner self?"

A little over-intellectualized, perhaps? How to reply?

Harper was an attractive girl, but it was hard to believe that a downtown law firm wanted to physically seduce her. But what else was the girl to think? Harper's grades were good, almost excellent, but she would never be a clerk to a Supreme Court Judge. Her senior year law bulletin article might be scholarly and have some insights, but she was not going to go down in history as a great legal thinker. Her personality was her strong point. Maybe they wanted to exploit that?

Maggie thought again that the job offer might be just another way to pressure herself about the mall project. Go along and your protégé's career will be assured. Or, the opposite: we will remove your friend from your office, if you don't cooperate.

Everything wasn't about herself. She had to think about what was best for Harper.

What Harper could certainly be would be an excellent lawyer for social causes. "I don't want to stand in your way of having a remarkable law career with a major firm. My offer still stands that I would help you start your own practice. The only one who can make this choice is you, and how you will feel about yourself. A career in the big leagues or a little, very satisfying, career. Most law students are never presented with these alternatives. I don't know what I would do if I were in your position."

Ash calling. "We lost him," he said.

"You lost who?" Or would that be "whom?" Ash always seemed to present these little quandaries.

"The Matalokus chauffeur. Dooley and I followed him after the usual charade where he picks up and delivers a phantom Matalokus to and from his business. Ten minutes later, he emerged from the sunken parking area under the mansion, walked to his own car and drove away for the evening."

"You followed him? Did he know you were behind him?"

"Maybe. Probably. Dooley was driving. Even I would know if Dooley was following me. Each time we lost him at a light, Dooley terrorized those drivers who got in between, swerved around them, even into oncoming lanes. Scared the crap out of me. Excuse my language."

What was it about her that prevented people from saying that already euphemistic word? Like she'd never heard anyone say a naughty word in all her life. Was this part of the aging business? That she'd become stern and sexless as the years robbed her of any possibility of being fun or having a sense of humor?

"Then what?" she asked.

"We lost him, but I'm pretty sure he was in a direct path to Brunswik. I hope that's important."

"You think this chauffeur might live in Brunswik?" Maggie was doubtful. She didn't feel like she was being given anything but conjecture. The chauffeur could have turned in any direction after losing them on the highway. All she was getting from Ash was a guess, supported only by his intuition. And men criticize women for following their instincts. "What are you going to do now, or are you telling me you're done with your investigation?"

"Not at all. Tomorrow, we're going to find a way to stop him and ask him questions. Dooley had a really good idea how we would do that."

"Since we aren't really talking and I will deny I ever had anything to do with the likes of you, could you tell me about this so-called idea?"

"We're going to crash into the rear end of the limo."

193

Chapter Thirty Four

Maggie sat in the plush middle chair reserved for the Mayor, behind the extended dais in the front of the council chambers. She was early as always and carefully read the agenda again, sometimes referring to the attached papers listing various items to be approved for purchase.

Only the camera man from the local cable channel was also present. He was in the glass-covered booth at the rear where his camera could catch every twitch and gesture of the council members.

Maggie liked to think of her pre-meeting reverie as the calm before the storm.

It wasn't the council members who made a fuss over an issue, she knew. Their usual decision was, of course, to follow the mayor's lead or to just take the recommendation of the City Manager. His job was to decide what should be done and the council's job to object only if there was a very good reason. The council did not want to, and had not the ability or expertise, to micromanage the city.

Their questions were only meant to placate some of their constituents about whatever issue was of current concern: the size of a sign, whether to accept a zoning variance recommendation, whether a new traffic signal would cause a snarl during rush hour.

Whatever objection that might have been raised by the council gadfly, Merit Berger, had been considered, taken seriously, and an effort had been made to placate him into agreement. He wasn't an obstructionist, just wanted to be heard, and usually the extra consideration satisfied him.

Actual aggravation usually came only from the audience of residents, primed by   local newspaper

194

reports and homeowner Internet sites to object or seek redress. No, the sign will be too big. No, a backyard swimming pool will change the character of the community. Why wasn't that street signal light already in place? Was the council waiting for just one more traffic death?

Maggie had been more nervous before meetings when she was just a mere councilperson. Unhappy with the pace of decision-making. Outraged by any effort to shove her to the side of a discussion. Hating that her suggestions for Agenda items were ignored.

Much better to be Mayor. In control. Able to get her way, if necessary. An eerie calmness would grip her during the meeting, as if something lacking in her life was being provided. As if energy flowed into her. She enjoyed being impossible to ignore.

The thought that her image was on television screens all over the city made her feel a little like Louise, a famous person. Someone everyone knew and, when she spoke, everyone paid attention. She's right, they would think, she's got a better grip on this than the others. Go, Maggie!

The frightening issue was number three on the agenda.

First was the approval of the minutes from the last meeting. Often, some councilman would quibble about the interpretation of his remarks, especially if he'd received feedback that he'd sounded like an idiot at the last meeting.

After would come the rote approval of purchases too small to demand attention.

Then old business. Finish up on some topic, throw in more money when original estimates for a project proved to be wishful thinking, do something quick before an error became a real embarrassment.

She'd had a moment of doubt where to put the mall issue.

In a way, it was old business, because a vote had already been made when the project was approved. In another way, it was new business, because, if the project were to go further, the Planning Commission would probably be asked to conduct a new study. Old business meant quick action, new meant continued delay.

When push came to shove, Maggie would be in trouble with somebody, either way.

Maggie remained ambiguous about the project. She didn't care whether the project continued or not, on the basis of what good it would do the city. She cared very much because her political career and the life of her grandchild now depended on the decision.

So she chose New Business, even if it would appear to some observers that this meant she was against the project. Speed before common sense?

One by one, aldermen and alderwomen arrived, nodded, shared information about their respective families, grew silent as they read the materials for the evening. Maggie's mind contained personal information about each on the council, knew their spouses and children's names. She went out of her way to be friendly with Merit Berger, which seemed to always disturb his equanimity.

The audience filled slowly. Prime seats were claimed.

Leaders of homeowner groups and others disgruntled personages stood at their seats to decide if their profiles would show well on the cable broadcast. They knew that, if enough interest on a speaker was anticipated, a cameraperson might come out of the booth and move to a designated area on the side of the dais to get a better angle from which to videograph.

Maggie recognized some of the faces and knew where they stood on the mall issue. Most of the audience appeared to be against the mall project. These were the same people who had objected in the meeting last May, the one prior to the approval of the project by the council in June.

Business owners were also represented, but not by their former spokesman, Severn Matalokus. This time it was a man who looked like a lawyer. He was dressed in an expensive suit and appeared to be slumming with the less enlightened. He undoubtedly would speak to the utter rationality of the project, trying to bend reality, whatever it was, to fit the desired effect. Only an idiot would be against the project, the attorney would imply, but not in those words.

Next to the lawyer, Maggie recognized the current chair of the Chamber of Commerce. She wondered if he might be one of those Republican businessmen who could be lured into running against her for State Senate. He'd always been very cordial to her in the past, but maybe that was a thin veneer hiding a spiteful and devious nature.

"Will the meeting please come to order," Maggie said, hitting her gavel once on dais. Immediately separate conversations between council members ceased, and the murmuring of the crowd faded out.

"We have a lot to do tonight and many people have signed up to speak, so let's get going." Maggie was known as a no-nonsense leader of meetings. "I'll entertain a motion to accept the minutes from the last meeting."

"So moved," the quietest of the council members said. He needed to get something on the record, so it wouldn't appear that he was hopelessly too shy to be in his position. Maggie wondered again why the poor man forced himself to be present. It must be some deep-seated desire to fulfill the aspirations of deceased parents, she decided.

No one objected to the acceptance of the minutes from the last meeting.

Papers shuffled as Maggie called for the motion to accept purchases. A motion was made and the matter was open for discussion. Each council member made a show of frowning, so that the audience would know they were working hard and not merely rubber stamping the purchases. Which they were.

One on the council, a tall man with a deep voice, asked for a clarification on one of the items. Were these fixtures up to industry standards? City Manager Tarko, from his seat to the side, provided some esoteric number to show that the fixture in question indeed met some standards set by some standard-setting company. The councilperson was satisfied with the answer and made no further comment.

"A motion to end discussion?" Maggie asked.

"So moved," said the mostly silent councilman.

"All in favor of ending discussion, say 'Aye.'" All so said.

"Discussion being closed, a vote on the motion to accept the purchases is in order. Those in favor say 'Aye.'" Maggie said. Hearing only Ayes, Maggie said, "The motion passes."

A short pause so councilpersons could shuffle their papers more, some so loudly the noise would be picked up and broadcast city-wide.

Maggie readied herself to announce "New Business," and then to specify that the subject of the mall project would be taken up. She moved her head away from the microphone to clear her throat.

She wanted to give a summary to bring everyone up to date. She hoped she could keep her own opinion out of the initial discussion, not wanting to criticize Severn's company, but only to voice the city's disappointment.

Maggie began, "As you all know, the project which was approved last June has somehow gone awry. We've lost contact with the building developer. It is our job to decide whether the project should proceed..."

A disturbance at the back of the council chambers. A mumbling by those nearest.

Maggie saw a disheveled and unshaven Rauptt, in uncharacteristic dirty jeans, rush into the room. For one horrible second, she saw what he was waving in his hands, and it wasn't a petition. A gun.

Rauptt leveled his gun in her direction. "I'm going to kill you, you goddamn bitch!"

The cameraman in the booth cursed. He couldn't get the image that would have appeared on the news that night in Brunswik and all of the Western World.

The shot was loud.

Maggie felt the gust of air pushed away by the hurling bullet.

Chapter Thirty-Five

Becky's report:

An attempted assassination of Brunswik Mayor Wellington by Planning Commission chairman Edgar Rauptt was thwarted yesterday, as the city council began debate on the future of a controversial mall project.

Rauptt was subdued and disarmed by Brunswik Chief of Police Feather after firing once in the direction of Mayor Wellington in the council chambers. Mayor Wellington was unhurt but Councilman Merit Berger suffered a non-life threatening wound and is resting comfortably at the Brunswik Hospital.

At the arraignment, Rauptt was charged with both attempted assassination and the alleged murder last Wednesday night of Oswalt Michaels, the prominent North Shore businessman and philanthropist.

Rauptt's whereabouts had been unknown since he went missing last week. Speculation now centers on the possibility Rauptt suffered some kind of mental breakdown, then emerged first to, allegedly, kill Michaels, then to assassinate Mayor Wellington.

Rauptt was known to be a strong supporter of the mall project and had brought the recommendation of the Planning Commission to the city council. The project was halted due to the apparent absence of its developer.

No animosity had been previously made public between Rauptt and Mayor Wellington. She had recently announced her intention to appoint him to fill the seat of the recently deceased councilman Gene Casey, who perished under suspicious circumstance during a fire at the site of the proposed mall.

Witnesses told this newspaper that Rauptt pushed his way into the council chambers and shouted "You g-d woman, you're going to die." Another witness quoted Rauptt as saying "You're not going to get away with this, you m-f." According to a third, Rauptt said "Sic semper tyrannis!" (Ever thus to tyrants!)

In an exclusive interview, Mayor Wellington, who is scheduled to be appointed as a State Senator by the governor later today, indicated surprise and bewilderment about Rauptt's actions.

"No one who ever met Mr. Rauptt would ever believe he could take such impetuous and unwise action. He was a very steady and reliable member and chairman of the Planning Commission, a rock in the community and example for others. I can only believe that something very wrong has occurred in his mental state, and I will mention him in my prayers."

Mayor Wellington also voiced concern over the injury of Councilman Berger, who, in the latest report, was in a stable condition with a superficial face wound. Family members indicated the wound looked like a fencing scar on his left cheek.

Post incident, Berger is being mentioned as a possible successor to Mayor Wellington, when she becomes a State Senator.

At an impromptu news conference after the council meeting was abruptly suspended, Chief Feather would not speculate why Rauptt would try to assassinate the Mayor. He said police intelligence had concluded, before the arraignment, that Rauptt must have been inside the Michaels mansion at the time of Michaels' death. No motive for that murder has yet been determined, he said.

Mrs. Wellington is in her third term as Mayor, and has not been a controversial mayor. She had been known as a hard worker whose only agenda is to, in the words of her campaign literature, "strengthen the services provided by the City of Brunswik and to keep its character as a good place to live and raise children."

Maggie sat behind a one-way mirror in the Brunswik police headquarters, watching and listening as

Chief Feather interrogated a shackled and handcuffed Rauptt.

He sat quietly with his head bowed forward. He made no attempt to be interested in the questions. Occasionally, he protested that he had answered a particular question about a hundred times before and he would no longer repeat answers.

Feather seemed unfazed by Rauptt's declining impulse to cooperate. In fact, Feather seemed energized, pleased to perform duties that didn't require him to sign papers. Trying to kill the Mayor elevated the attempted crime into legendary proportions. Feather relished the idea of being part of a Brunswik legend, the police chief who questioned the murderer and assassin.

Rauptt finally had enough of Feather's yammering. He drew back into a more rigid position on his chair, looked Feather in the eyes, and said simply, "You want to know why? Mayor Wellington ruined my life."

Maggie's interest focused. How had she ruined Rauptt's life? If that's what he meant.

"She robbed me of my success. She stole from me my golden opportunity. She deserves to die."

Maggie tried to remember if she had recently robbed and stolen. If she had, wouldn't there be a net increase in her assets? Something to show for all that robbing and stealing? Something tangible? Instead, she was short one grandchild.

"Do you know what it means to have your life ruined, destroyed?" Rauptt asked.

Maggie mentally answered the question in the affirmative.

Actually, an easy question to answer. Everyone's life is ruined. Oh, there may be some who seem completely happy, who have fulfilled their every goal, but wasn't that just an illusion?

Whose life hadn't been ruined? By disease, disability, death? Early loss of a parent that leaves you unprotected from the world's harshness? The death of a spouse that leaves you alone?

What about being born talentless and less than brilliant, or having a flaw in your brain that forever impedes your ability to cope with the ordinary challenges of life?

How about being born homely or lacking in personal attributes, so you must struggle while the beautiful, handsome and athletic easily succeed? What, you say you are short, fat, or ugly, or a combination of two or all three?

How many lives are buffeted by things beyond an individual's control? How about the wars that take your life and the lives of your loved ones, or the economic cycles that destroy your business? Floods and mudslides? Hurricanes and tornadoes? Fires that leave charred ashes?

The unlucky remain luckless, the impoverished remain poor.

Get over it. Do the best you can. Realize that no one survives life without scars and resentments. That the world wasn't designed for you. That no one really cares whether you are happy or not, except the few who share your life.

Get a dog, get a cat that loves you as you are. Don't expect the world to give you unconditional love.

Maggie's reverie was interrupted by Rauptt. "My own sister. Why did I ever listen to her?"

"Your sister?" Feather repeated. "What about her?"

"It was all her idea. She's the guilty one you ought to be arresting."

"Fine. Just tell me where she is and I'll do just that. You say she helped you in your plotting and planning? Accessory to your crimes?"

Rauptt was near tears. Maggie hardly recognized Rauptt's anguished face, so different from the one that she'd seen in the restaurant, preening in his success and expertise.

Reserve gone, words poured out.

"Yes," he said. "Not just the accessory. The architect of it all, because she couldn't control her impulses, wanted it all, couldn't be satisfied, let nothing get in her way. I'm the accessory. She's the perpetrator. It was all her."

Feather frowned. "You're starting to talk in riddles. Would you care to clarify what you mean? First of all where is your sister?"

"You like riddles? She's still where I could be at her beck and call. Still there beneath me but always over me."

Riddles, Maggie thought. Oh, good! I'm good at those. Let's see. At her beck and call but always beneath but over.

Physically there close by, but beneath but over him? Maybe he means physically below but dominating him? Telling him what to do. Ever present. Living near or on top of him? Or beneath him.

Such as having a home on top of him or beneath him?

Rauptt lived in a condominium building, Maggie remembered. She'd explored his condo herself. There were condos above and below his. Sometimes, Maggie knew, people who are very rich buy the condo above or below and connect them with a staircase so they can double their living space or accommodate a relative.

Had there been a door she hadn't found in Rauptt's condo that led to a stairway that led to his sister? Maybe. There had been a door in an inappropriate place off one hallway. She'd looked inside, but had she seen the back wall? Clothes were in the way, stored, like winter outfits that would be taken out when the snow began to fall.

Where was Smith? Maggie wanted to explore that closet.

Chapter Thirty-Six

"You see a connection?" Smith asked. "You think that Rauptt's sister is Mrs. Matalokus and that she might have Ethan?"

"Yes," Maggie said. The evening was chill but Maggie still felt overheated. She'd decided to wear her fall jacket to hide the uncomfortable and unattractive bullet-proof vest provided by Chief Feather.

They sped along in a police squad car, its headlights causing brighter cones in the darkness, but without the siren screaming and throbbing. Even so, motorists gave them the right of way as soon as they realized a policeman was behind them. At least people are driving slower because of our presence, Maggie thought.

Smith remained skeptical. "I'm not so sure you're right. The girl in the picture at Rauptt's condo looks a little like the older woman at the council meeting, I agree, and somewhat like the picture on Mrs. Matalokus' driver's license. But, you know, facial similarities can show up on non-relatives. And sometimes memory plays tricks. Did you look at the pictures at the same time you looked at the video, trying to identify common features or to rule them out?"

Maggie shook her head.

"Besides, people see what they want to see," the young man said. "You wanted to see similarities.

"I'm relying on my memory, which usually serves very well. I'm good at remembering faces. All good politicians are. The same nose was in the video and in Rauptt's picture and Mrs. Matalokus' license. I also saw this woman again at a restaurant and got a good look at her. In any case, I'm certain enough to want to search Rauptt's condo again, and make sure there's no clue we missed that would help us to find Mrs. Matalokus. You know what's at stake."

"I know." He frowned deeply. Smith must have felt very guilty about not yet finding Maggie's grandchild. "I'm sure we'll find Ethan very soon. I don't think anyone expects the mall project to go through now. Whoever is holding him might just give up."

Doubtful. Maggie took a deep breath.

If Rauptt had acted alone, her grandchild was locked somewhere awaiting Rauptt's return. He'd never be released to retrieve Ethan. Might never be found.

Really not much better a situation, if Ethan was with Mrs. Matalokus. Wouldn't the woman be just as angry as Rauptt that their plans had failed? And she might take out her anger on Ethan.

Maggie shifted position uncomfortably, not wanting to share her fears with Smith.

Instead, she shared another of her conclusions. "I think Rauptt owns the mall property, don't you?"

"Must. He must have bought up the property and then brought in the Matalokus company. That still doesn't mean that he's Severn Matalokus' brother-in-law."

"It does in my mind," Maggie said.

Their destination reached, Smith parked the squad in an illegal tow-away zone in front of the condo building. "Nobody's going to bother a police car," Smith said. "It's perfectly legitimate to inspect Rauptt's condo again, now that he's implicated in who knows what kind of fraud and murder."

Maggie experienced a *deja vu* feeling to be back at the condo building, or was it a recurring nightmare feeling? She also felt as if her muscles had been clenched for quite a while. In fact, since the shot whizzed past her at the council meeting. Words reverberated oddly in her ears. She felt heavy and walking was an effort. Time had slowed down.

They traveled up the elevator to Rauptt's floor. Maggie hadn't told Smith her theory of connected condo units, fearing he would also pick it apart, criticize it for being so unlikely.

Maggie understood the problems they'd face if they tried to check the condo's above and below Rauptt's. Unfortunately, they'd need warrants or, at least, the permission of the condo's legal agent to get into those condos. Of course, she could always stand with her ear at each condo door, above and below, listening for Ethan's voice. As odd an image as that presented to her imagination.

Smith used to key he'd brought from the police station to open the door to Rauptt's condo. They entered silently. Maybe someone was in the condo?

Smith had a moment of doubt. He placed his hand inside his jacket, close to the gun he carried in a holster. His impulse was to grab his gun. Police procedure demanded that he be ready to fire back if someone attacked them. "Do you mind if I draw my gun?" he asked Maggie. "Would it upset you so soon after being fired upon?"

She thought about what he'd asked. "No, probably reassure me, if anything." Smith led forward with his gun held in front of him.

Her mind was already off the subject of guns and onto the business of searching. Lights on, her eyes focused into detailed observational mode. What was out of place? What was not there that should have been?

She examined the carpet in the inner hallway, noted the colors on the walls, the patterns in the wallpaper. Some taste decisions were clearly inappropriate. Not so surprising in a condo decorated by a man.

Maggie supposed some of the knick-knacks she saw were meant by Rauptt to be reassuringly masculine. A miniature of a baseball park, the one in St. Louis. A picture of a nude woman, suffering from exposure, poor thing.

"What are we looking for specifically?" Smith asked.

"I won't know until I see it." Maggie moved quickly to the hallway closet where she'd imagined a secret staircase could be hidden. She pushed away the clothes. No, the wall seemed solid.

Her memory of every haunted house movie she'd ever watched came back to her. She looked for hidden panels and secret switches that would cause the back wall to spin around. Nothing.

"I want to look carefully at each room," she said. "Slowly and carefully."

Smith nodded.

They went into the small bedroom. Maggie inspected the closet, but again saw no possible place for a stairway entry.

Men's bedrooms tell a lot about them, Maggie thought. Rauptt really was obsessively neat. His closet was so well organized, his shoes were hung, two by two, like animals ready to go on Noah's ark.

First into the kitchen, Maggie saw a sliding double door. Probably this was a pantry for dry goods, some pots and pans and appliances. She pushed the sliding doors open and observed that half of the wall had no shelves. Where no packages were kept, was a door.

Maggie closed the double door quickly and waited for Smith to enter. "I think I just heard a knock on the front door," she said.

"Are you sure?" Smith asked. "I didn't hear anything and my hearing's pretty good."

"Yes. Definitely. Men aren't as good as women in hearing high pitched sounds."

"Wouldn't a knock be in the lower hearing range?" Smith asked.

"Just check the door, please."

Smith exited the kitchen. Maggie thought she'd have at least a minute and a half without Smith while he checked the front door. She opened the double doors of the pantry and looked at the inner door. Did it have a lock?

Yes, but the door wasn't locked. She opened it wide and looked down into a dark expanse. Someone could blunder through that door and plunge downward. Maybe she should wait for Smith or search for a flashlight in the kitchen drawers?

She took an experimental step through the door. A light, obviously triggered by motion, flashed on, blinding her momentarily.

A circular staircase. It didn't look new and it didn't seem sturdy. Under ordinary circumstances, she would have hesitated to travel down those narrow steps.

She had to find out what was downstairs.

Maggie turned before descending and closed the double door, then the door to the stairs. No need to endanger Smith. If anyone would be hurt because of her curiosity, it would be her.

She unconsciously found the best way to distribute her weight and keep her balance while moving in a descending spiral around the center pole of the staircase.

Just as she was becoming dizzy and her hand began to strain from holding on tight to whatever surface she could grab, she reached the bottom.

From above, she heard the muffled sound of Smith calling out. "Where are you?"

He won't find the door in the pantry for a few minutes, she thought. Until he can search the whole condo and comes back, frustrated, to examine the kitchen more carefully.

Maggie found a door similar to the one above. This one also had a lock. She tested the door and found that this lock also had not been engaged.

The door swung open slowly. Maggie saw another double pantry door. So the stairwell began and ended in the respective kitchens of the above and below condos.

Maggie ventured forth, sticking her head just beyond the pantry. The kitchen was not lit, but moonlight came through a window.

She heard a high pitched child's voice.

Chapter Thirty-Seven

Relief mixed with fear. If the voice she'd heard was Ethan's, at least he was still alive. Alive and in danger.

Maggie moved forward into the lower condo's kitchen, trying to make no noise as she walked on the thick white slate tile. Whoever lived here had invested wisely in flooring. Good flooring really makes a difference. Maggie wondered if this condo had inlaid wooden floors in the bedrooms and hallways. Maybe she should install those in hers? It's said that parquet gives the floor a warmer texture.

A possible mental map of the condo flashed into her consciousness. Was this condo laid out the same as the one above? Most likely, but not necessarily. People do move walls if they are not weight-bearing, the walls not the people. No reason, if you've got the space of two condos, that you can't break through the walls of one to make, for instance, an immense family room or whatever. That's what she would do.

Maggie considered buying the downstairs condo in her building, if it came up for sale. Her own condo, while adequate for one, might not be adequate if she ever remarried. Of course, one has to still be alive if one remarries. "Harold, I'm still alive. Marry me and we'll expand to downstairs and you can make a bowling alley."

Maggie went through the opening into the dining room. Her suspicions were correct. Former owners had greatly expanded this room to allow for a very long table. If Mrs. Matalokus had any friends, she could have had a wonderful dinner party.

Maggie saw a corridor leading out of the dining room. She wondered how many people had been called to dinner and walked through that corridor with visions of roast beef dancing in their heads.

Beyond, she guessed, must be an open area, a family room with lots of leather couches and chairs or a more formal living room with pictures purchased from fine galleries. Certainly a hutch for family treasures.

Maggie thought of her own keepsake cabinet. She knew exactly which of her daughters should get which item, when the inevitable occur.

If she were to die now, without preamble, the items might not be distributed exactly according to her preferences. Her grandmother's tea kettle should go to Tracy, as the oldest, and to compensate, the candlesticks from Greece should go to Kim. What if, after she was gone, the reverse occurred?

She really needed to get her will updated. She could update it herself but didn't feel so confident anymore about estate planning, having forgotten at least half she'd learned in law school and not being up to date on current case law.

A course would be offered by the Illinois Bar Association on the subject next year, and she ought to take it. This course would count towards the continuing education requirements for lawyers in Illinois. Usually she took those courses on-line every other year. It might be more fun to be in a real-life class again, surrounded by people she knew and who knew her. Maybe she'd find a man she'd like more than Harold?

Maggie began to walk down the corridor. At the class, she decided, she would ask a question about disinheritance.

Why had that popped into her head? Severn and his brother had been rivals for their father's affections. How did that play out in their father's will? Had one son been disinherited?

"Just shut up, you little brat."

As Maggie entered a long room with multiple pieces of furniture, she saw Mrs. Matalokus, at the far end, holding Ethan by his non-broken arm. A gun was in the woman's other hand, the one not holding Maggie's grandson. "I'm sure I heard someone walking around. No it's not your mother. It can't be my stupid brother

211

either. He's in jail. You know, Ethan, you are bad company. All this whimpering. Suck it up. I'm not going to hurt you unless it's really necessary."

Comforting words. Mrs. Matalokus, a woman of indeterminate age, looked miffed, as if the delivery man was late, had not arrived within the promised two hour window. So inconvenient.

Maggie recognized the woman's nose. This was certainly who she'd expected. Smith had been wrong and Maggie had been right. See, I told you.

How much longer before Smith followed her down? A few minutes, a few seconds. She hadn't heard any noise behind her.

"Don't try to hide. I see you, you witch," Mrs. Matalokus said. Well, Maggie thought, at least the woman isn't as profane as her brother. It was a promotion to go from bitch to witch.

"May I call you Olivia? I feel like we're old friends. I saw you at the fast food restaurant recently. Did you know it was me?"

"Was that you? All I saw was a midget-sized old woman in clown make-up."

Apparently, her offer of friendship with Olivia had been rejected. "What are you planning to do with my grandson? Why don't you just let him go? I'll leave, and you'll have some time to run away before the police arrive."

"A generous offer, but, no. I think that as long as I have the spawn of the mayor's daughter, that I have the upper hand."

"Not really. You can't hold him here forever. I'd take the chance of getting away. There's nothing you can do about the mall project now. Am I right that your brother owns the property?"

"No, I own the property."

Maybe Maggie could get some more information. "Where is Severn, your husband or former husband?"

Her gun made jerky motions as she spoke. "He's late."

212

What did that mean? Late, as in my late husband? Or had lost track of the time?

On a roll, question-wise, Maggie asked. "Was it you who pushed Ethan off the slide when he broke his arm?"

"No. That was my idiot brother. He was trying to snatch the brat and fumbled it. What else would you like to know?"

"Did Rauptt kill Michaels?"

"Yes, he'd been kidnapped by Michaels' people and held in that fortress of his. My brother finally figured out that he could force the door open. Michaels was a good man, dead."

Can't argue with her there, Maggie thought.

What else? "Was it Michaels who owned the big shopping mall just beyond the Brunswik border? Is that what the fight was all about? Not wanting to lose a few shoppers?"

"Michaels and some other very well placed investors. Hey, we're talking about money here."

Both were silent for an extended period.

Maggie asked, "What are you going to do?"

She saw indecision on Olivia's face. First deciding she would keep Ethan as a hostage, then deciding to run, then redeciding to stand her ground. In an instant, coming to another conclusion. "I'm going to release the boy, if you promise you'll personally take no legal action against us. Like you won't be the complainant."

This woman really needs legal advice, Maggie thought. Not having a complainant wouldn't stop any state prosecution. Olivia would be in just as much legal trouble either way as the accessory to murder and attempted murder, not to mention kidnapping.

On the other hand, Olivia got some points for not wanting to kill Ethan. Killing children must be the outer limit of how far she will go, Maggie thought. Makes sense. Most of the rest of the civilized women in the world would stop at just murdering adults.

"I'll do what you said, just release his arm. I'll try not to do anything that will add to your woes."

213

Olivia released Ethan. He ran to his grandmother. She embraced him briefly and put him behind her. "Run, honey. Go to the kitchen. A nice man, Smith, will be there soon."

Ethan ran down the corridor. She should have said something about the hidden door. Ethan would really be surprised when Smith emerged from the pantry. A team of psychologists would need to work hard so that every time Ethan saw a pantry, he didn't pee in his pants.

Suzanne could reassure the child, counsel him, and he'll probably reach adulthood with only a slight stutter.

"What are you going to do now?" Maggie asked.

"I'm going to do what you said and run. I might get away, you know, but I'll still have my revenge on you. You'll never know where I'll be. Even if I don't get away, I have ways, even in prison, to make sure you will never feel safe again. You'll be looking over your shoulder the rest of your life, wondering if you or your family is in danger."

Maggie remained silent, thinking. Olivia was correct. As long as this woman is alive, she and her family wouldn't be safe. How many of Olivia's "friends" would be willing to act on her behalf, even if she were in prison? A good place to solicit for a murderer. Olivia probably had a lot of money hidden away somewhere and could pay for someone to do the murderous deed. Olivia could take her time to exact her revenge.

"I believe you." Maggie said.

She took out Feather's gun from her pocket, aimed, and shot Olivia Matalokus between the eyes.

Chapter Thirty-Eight

Report by Becky:

An alleged co-conspirator in the attempt on Brunswik Mayor Wellington's life was killed in a gunfight yesterday by Police Superintendent Mort Feather.

Olivia Matalokus, the sister of Sidney Rauptt, who attempted to kill Mayor Wellington Thursday evening during a city council meeting, was fatally injured Friday morning by Chief Feather in her Brunswik condominium. Mrs. Matalokus was pronounced dead on arrival at Brunswik Hospital.

Chief Feather reported that he and a Brunswik detective, Marcus Smith, were searching Rauptt's condo after the attempted assassination, when they heard a disturbance in the condo below. Investigation revealed the presence of Mrs. Matalokus, the wife of a developer who was deeply involved in a controversial mall project,

Mrs. Matalokus drew her gun and attempted to kill both Chief Feather and Detective Smith, according to the police report. She was shot in the upper torso, according to Chief Feather, after he gave her a warning to stand down and she began unmistakable gestures to pull the trigger of her gun.

"This is unfortunate," Chief Feather told this newspaper exclusively, "but was a choice she made. To fight, rather than to surrender and face justice with her brother, who is accused of multiple crimes, including the alleged murder of real estate magnate Oswalt Michaels.

Rauptt may also be charged with real estate fraud in misrepresenting his role in a mall project while chairman of the city's Planning Commission.

215

The Assistant State's Attorney assigned to Rauptt's prosecution asserted in a news conference Friday morning, that Rauptt was the owner of most of the property to be used for the mall project in Brunswik. It is speculated that Rauptt attacked Mayor Wellington because of her opposition to the project.

Mrs. Matalokus was a North Shore resident, who apparently had few social connections. The Matalokus' maintained a spacious estate but little is known about her life prior to or after moving into the area.

Severn Matalokus, her husband, is unavailable for comment. He has been unreachable by city officials for months, according to Brunswik City Manager H.B. Tarko.

No statement was issued by Severn Matalokus' real estate development company, nor have any Matalokus family representatives come forward.

Chief Feather, who came to Brunswik after a distinguished career in law enforcement, explained his presence at the scene of the subsequent shooting, on the basis of the high profile of the investigation.

"I could not delegate a matter of this importance," he told this reporter. Chief Feather declined to discuss his prior successes in face to face confrontations with armed assailants, indicating that any comment might prejudice current or unresolved cases.

Chief Feather is married to the former Elise Bergen. They have two children.

Rauptt's attorney said that he would fight all charges . . .

So long as Rauptt has any money left, Maggie thought, completing the sentence.

This was the best way: to give Feather the credit or blame. After all, it was his gun she'd used to kill Mrs. Matalokus. And Feather so desperately wanted to show the world what a tough guy he is.

Maggie sat at her desk in City Hall, having told her secretary that she did not want to be disturbed. She was recently returned from Springfield, where to the praise of all, she'd been appointed State Senator by the Governor.

Maggie had not even been required by the delegation of successful politicians to assert her opposition to the mall project. Apparently, almost getting killed by someone who thought she was against the project is sufficient evidence of political fealty and faithfulness.

Letter of Olivia Matalokus, to be opened in case of her death, and purchased for $200 from the Matalokus chauffeur by Ash.

If this is being read, then I am dead.

I am not writing to supply the curious with reasons for my actions. Suffice it to say that things have happened to me in my life that more than justify anything I've done. I regret nothing and would have taken the same actions if given a second chance.

Let me begin by saying my maiden name is not Rauptt. My brother and I adopted that name as a means of psychologically separating ourselves from our parents and backgrounds. Why "Rauptt" you ask? Why the two "T's"? I can only answer, why not?

I was married, just once, to Severn Matalokus, a good boy but a very dull man. I took pity on him. He needed my beauty. He was badly flawed, and I still don't know why his father so favored him over his brother, Anthony. His father left all his estate to Severn, thereby sharply admonishing Anthony for reasons no one ever understood. Perhaps Anthony reminded the old man of his old man.

Personally, I found Anthony to be a very bad boy and a very exciting man. When the glow of the marriage ceremony with Severn wore off, and take it from me, it wore off quickly, I found myself intrigued by my brother-in-law.

It wasn't because of his looks. I have to tell you that both brothers were nearly identical, except for their personalities. Anthony was smart and sexy, and Severn, as I said, was dull.

Anthony and I engaged in our first sexual encounter in a pantry where I had gone to find some more ketchup, assisted by Anthony. We were quick about it and neat and no one suspected when we rejoined the party in the dining room of the mansion. Severn never suspected, less because we were so stealthy than because he could not conceive of the possibility of his wife's adultery. As I said, he was dull and this included a lack of imagination.

Severn would never have divorced me. He didn't believe in divorce and would have fought it. I would never get all of Severn's fortune if I just divorced him and there would have been quite a scandal if I married my former brother-in-law. In any case, marrying Anthony made no sense at the time, because he was poor. Everything was in Severn's name.

So Anthony and I killed Severn and put his body in the trunk of Anthony's car. Anthony switched wallets with Severn.

Anthony then anonymously told the police where Severn could be found. He represented himself as Severn and identified Severn's body as his own. I backed him up, identifying the body as Anthony's as well.

Am I explaining this sufficiently? Anthony took Severn's identify and money and me, of course, his wife.

You may wonder, did I feel guilty about sleeping with Anthony or the charade after his murder? The answer is no.

Unable to stay in St. Louis, where surely some idiot would eventually have detected the difference in the identities, even of the near twins, we quickly moved as husband and wife to the Chicago area, the North Shore, specifically.

Anthony had no problem using Severn's money, since to the world, he was Severn. We bought a mansion and Anthony again went into the real estate development business, for which he had a talent.

We prospered and, I suppose we were as happy as any couple who had committed murder. Unfortunately, Anthony, being a bad boy, took a shine to a whore down at work.

I don't want anyone to think that I did not consider the possibility of just killing the whore rather than Anthony, but it occurred to me that I would end up with a disgusting serial cheater if Anthony remained alive. After all, he had cheated with both me and the whore.

The tipping point came when I read Anthony's will. The bastard left me nothing. All his money would go to charity after his death. Apparently, Anthony had some guilty qualms after all about what he had done to his brother.

I could have claimed the widow's share if Anthony died, but the bastard had also left a letter with his attorney admitting to his replacement of his brother in my bed if I challenged the disinheritance.

Here was the essence of my problem. I wasn't Anthony's widow. Illinois does not allow common-law marriage, according to a lawyer I consulted. And claiming I was Severn's widow would have put me on death row.

And to further complicate things, get this: Anthony had found a way to remove the marriage certificate of Severn and myself from the public record. How, I don't know. Money talks and honesty walks. But why go to the trouble? Apparently, and this is the only thing I can imagine, he didn't want anyone to compare Severn's signature on the marriage license to his. A bit of paranoia, I suppose, or did he somehow think this was another way to disinherit me? That I wasn't even Severn's widow?

Also, I need to tell you that my brother, Edgar, who earned his living by blackmailing Anthony and me, pushed through a mall project as chairman of the Brunswik Planning Commission. This was according to Anthony's plan.

So, naturally, when my brother and I killed Anthony, we kept it a secret so his will couldn't be probated and we could continue with the highly profitable mall plan. I sent a limo every day to Matalokus Holdings. Keeping the death a secret gave us enough time to transfer the title to the mall properties from Anthony's dummy corporation to our dummy corporation.

219

Where is Anthony's body? My brother and I had no problem disposing of it in Lake Michigan, where all bad little boys end up.

The rest you know. Things did not work out. The Mayor of Brunswik took it upon her little clown self to stand in our way and ruin us.

If I am dead, Maggie Wellington killed me, metaphorically speaking.

The End

Other books by Leon Shure:

The Brunswik Mysteries
Rehearsal for Murder
Littlemayor
Panic Parade
Collected in The Brunswik Mystery Trilogy

Vanek Mysteries
Screams and Bleeds
Think Fast, Detective Vanek
See Here, Detective Vanek
Collected in:
The Vanek Trilogy

The Cal Hodges Mysteries
The Search for Hanson Sted
Deathbed Confession
River Cruise Murders
Collected in:
The Cal Hodges Mystery Trilogy
Dr. Adam Karl Mysteries
The Baba Yaga

I.S. Blut Mysteries
Crone's Bones

The Wilberforce Mysteries
Wedding Party Murders

Coming Soon: Presumed Alive

#Conversationstoppers: Puns, *Non Sequiturs*, and Impossible Scenarios
#Conversationstoppers 2: More Puns, *Non Sequiturs*, and Impossible Scenarios
#Conversationstoppers 3: Even More Puns, *Non-Sequiturs*, and Impossible Scenerios
Visit my Twitter page at http://twitter.com/slistack

**The Search for Hanson Sted,
a Cal Hodges Mystery**
by
Leon Shure
Copyright 2017
By Leon Shure

Chapter One

"What we're talking about, Mr. Hodges," Trisha said, "is money and lots of it."

Cal Hodges, chief investigator for the law firm of Benson, Benson and Farley, smiled. He got the joke. Usually clients claimed the most praise-worthy of motives, but underneath it all was money and the pursuit thereof.

Refreshing to hear such honesty. But he wondered if, behind the cynicism, she was hiding something. His job was to find out the hidden.

He had about 5 heartbeats to react with a spoken reply. He'd been told often that his slow, deliberative style of conversation bothered clients. But he needed a moment to get a fuller impression of his new client.

Stalling, he shifted in his upholstered chair, jiggling the assignment sheet provided by the firm for each new case, hearing the paper crinkle. He gave Trisha a longer look. She sat in the chair in front of his desk, with her back very straight. An orderly woman, each hair in place, a contrast to the chaos of his office with its thrown about papers and files that would never be filed.

A question in his mind. Trisha Sted, by reputation, already had a lot of money. Her family had been clients for three generations, according to the assignment sheet Cal held between his finger and his thumb. That meant, what the sheet was implying was, be nice to this woman, her family had enriched the partners.

No need to warn me to be nice, he thought, I'm nice to everyone. Maybe not everyone. Actually, not nice to anyone. Just civil. Usually civil. Not exactly known for my civility, but civil underneath, secretly civil.

Silence stretched as long as he could without, hopefully, being openly rude, he said "I understand." Which was what he said to all new clients, whether he understood what they wanted or not. He would eventually understand, which was enough. By the time he was done, he'd understand way too much.

"Do you really? I'm glad." She smiled back at him. But beneath the smile, her expression and narrowed eyes said, if make-up could talk, don't even try to fool me. The woman knew when she was being trifled with. Cal readjusted his evaluation of Ms. Sted to also include intelligence.

Contrary to her reputation. A bubble-head, so far as the media was concerned. Famous for being famous, everything she did was duly noted and reported to a breathless transfixed public. Researching her public image would be easy, but what about her real self?

Because he suspected she had a real self. Cal wrote on the assignment sheet "Real?" with a question mark in case he was proven wrong. Unlikely, but the possibility always existed. He could be very wrong. The investigation isn't over until the opposite conclusion is examined was his motto.

"I've written it all down so I don't forget anything," Trisha said. She drew a sheet of paper from her purse. When she tipped the top of the letter forward to move her fingers down the edges, Cal could see that the page was typed.

Did Trisha do her own typing? Had she dictated to a secretary or to a computer program? If she did her

223

own work, it meant whatever she really wanted from him was important to her.

"Are you going to leave that with me?"

She looked at him with some surprise. "If you want. Is that your standard practice?"

A woman who does not suffer salesclerks gladly. "Yes." Cal didn't offer an explanation. Sometimes what people wrote, and how they wrote it, gave him some real insights, even clues. He was afraid if he explained too much, she wouldn't give him the page.

A twinkly, friendlier smile, from Ms. Trisha. A reaction to his short reply, he thought. Was she afraid that he wasn't entranced with her, not coming under her spell? She was a very beautiful woman, although he didn't know yet how much was artifice, how much from nature.

"My brother, Hanson," she read, "disappeared on" she gave the date. Winter almost four years before. "His car was found at Mallard Park Lake in unincorporated Barringame Township, Illinois."

Was such beauty a drawback, a limitation, a hardship? Did it dominate her every conversation with others? Such women, Cal thought, must never develop the conversation skills of a normal or average looking woman. A beautiful person probably doesn't know how to focus on someone else. There must also be other drawbacks, problems of the very attractive, but for the moment, he couldn't think of any.

She continued. "Hanson was never found, just blood that proved to be his."

"By DNA?"

"Yes. Hanson was never heard of again. No reports of sightings. No use of credit cards. Nothing." She looked up, waiting for a question.

"I presume the police investigated and found nothing."

"Correct. My mother also hired several professional investigators who were unable to find out anything about his whereabouts."

"You were working under the presumption that he was alive?"

Surprised, a bit confused by his question. "Yes, of course. We hoped he had only been injured, attacked but still alive, and was in hiding."

On these bare facts, Cal was doubtful. Injured people usually find their way to hospitals. The dead can't be healed. Also, investigations go cold very quickly. Her brother hadn't been found soon after the discovery of the abandoned car, so the chances were good he'd never be found. "I don't understand then, what you want from me," Cal said. "Sounds like you've investigated his disappearance in every possible way."

She took a breath, made an involuntary shake of her head. A warding off gesture. Some guilt here, some real unhappiness here? Or some realistic acting, he thought. "Now we need to prove he's dead."

"Why?"

"It's all down on the paper here, but the reason is that my grandmother died. She left her entire estate to Hanson and me. Hanson has not been missing so long that he can be declared legally dead. We need that money, all of it, now. Business reversals, that kind of thing."

Why did the inheritance skip a generation? Trisha had only mentioned her mother as the one hiring investigators. Did that mean her father was deceased or just out of the picture, perhaps divorced or estranged? Also, why didn't Trisha's mother inherit Sted Industries when her husband died? The estate must have reverted to the paternal grandmother for some reason. Was it marital discord between the parents, or bad blood between Trisha's mother and the grandmother, or estate planning to prevent an ill-equipped widow from ruining the family business?

Cal stopped his speculations. A lot of guesswork based on nothing, Cal thought.

He leaned back in his chair. If this lady wanted him to launch another fruitless search, he was fine with it. He would check with Stuart Benson, the managing partner and his mentor. What were the legal reasons for this investigation? What kind of definitive findings would allow a court to make a declaration of death short of the statutory time, seven years missing?

"I've given this some thought," Trisha said. Cal was sure she had. "And an investigation would be a problem, given my . . . fame." The word she was looking for was notoriety, Cal thought. But she was right. Any mention of her name would bring out the paparazzi in people. Calls to the radio news lines, pictures snapped by cell phones, videos downloaded to the internet receiving a million hits in the first hour. "I'm just saying that we'd have to come up with a cover story."

"I'm listening," he said. Cal slouched forward, his own defensive gesture. A problem of being in the presence of such beauty, he thought, is the feeling, that, in comparison, one's own charms must be very feeble, even diminished by comparison. Cal didn't spend a great deal of time worrying about his looks, but now he felt his nose was too big, his tall frame kind of stooped. He was the opposite of a pretty boy. Usually a good thing.

She pursed her beautiful lips. "I've discussed this with Stuart. His suggestion was to create an agency, draw up the papers, which he said would not be difficult, to create an agency that searched for missing persons."

Cal looked doubtful. Where was she going with this?

She continued. "An agency that sought out people who have disappeared, representing families of lost souls after the police had given up. An agency that never stops looking. My brother could just be one of many still being investigated. You could make up some business cards, appear to be searching for generic missing persons, contact the local police with a good story. And have someone, like Stuart, vouch for you."

Actually, not a bad idea. Cal wondered how much of this proposed agency was suggested by Stuart and how much came from Trisha.

"Here are the reports from the investigators we hired." She handed Cal a large file, probably supplied to her after her meeting with Stuart.

Was the meeting over? Trisha gathered herself together, leaned forward, and fished below Cal's line of sight to find her purse.

But she hadn't told him anything about her brother yet. "Could you answer a few more questions before you go?"

She sat back, but tentatively, ready to begin her ascent again as soon as possible. "I'm sorry, I thought we were done. I have to run now. Another appointment, you know?"

"Fine, if you must go. Maybe that would be for the best. I'll do the basic research, read the reports you've given me, then come to see you at your home, if that's alright. "

A little hesitant. Was there something about her home that she didn't want him to see? Had they fired the butler because of the business reversals couldn't be covered by half an inheritance?

"I wonder," she said, "if it wouldn't just be easier if you came to the house this weekend? We're having some people, mostly friends, over for a brainstorming session about a new product I want to introduce. You would just be another of the overnight guests. You could meet my family and friends in a less pressured, more informal, way. Use our cover story." She must have sensed that Cal was less than enthusiastic. Cal didn't think of himself as a social animal. "You could bring whoever you want, your wife or significant other."

He could bring Merle. That put a whole new face on the prospect. "I think that would be helpful. I accept your invitation."

What should he say next? Cal realized he didn't know the first thing about arranging a weekend stay. "If you don't mind, I'll give your number to my fiancé. She's an attorney for the firm. Merle Grayson. She can make the arrangements." A moment of doubt. What if Merle didn't want to join him for a weekend on the job? "I'll be there for sure, but I'll have to find out if she's available. I know she's free on Saturday night."

They always were together on Saturday nights, their permanent date night for the last year. His concern was that Merle had specifically asked him to set aside time this weekend to revise plans for their upcoming wedding. She might even consider this weekend invitation to be a deliberate distraction. But no need to share these concerns with Trisha, he decided. He was uncomfortable talking about himself.

When Trisha was gone, he sat motionless for a long time, thinking, tapping his pen on his desk to some random cadence. Trisha had surprised him in a number of ways.

He let all she'd said float up into his consciousness, not trying to sort the information out. He often did this. The most important facts would come to mind first, of their own volition.

What was it she'd said about the missing? She'd called them "lost souls." Her brother was a lost soul. That was the "realist" thing she'd said.

Somewhere her brother was. Perhaps so changed he was unrecognizable. Either alive or in the grave amouldering.

Would Trisha wish someday she'd never asked him to find her brother?

Made in the USA
Monee, IL
06 April 2022

94284189R00135